A
COWBOY
CHRISTMAS

by

MICHAEL J. MOORE

Dedicated to my mother,
whose love of romantic holiday movies
inspired me to write this book.

And to my father,
as some of the many lessons he taught me
are represented within these pages.

Other books by Michael J. Moore

ROBERT LOWE: An Origin Story
THE TALES OF ROBERT LOWE

Cover art by Britton Mitchell
Photography by Michael J. Moore

PROLOGUE

Her eyes fluttered open briefly. How long had she been asleep? It didn't matter. She needed to wake up and in the brief moment she had opened her eyes, she saw the face she most wanted to see. After several moments, her eyes opened fully and she found herself gazing upon the love of her life. His expression conveyed love, concern, hope, and admiration all at once. How did he manage to show so much of what he was feeling with just his stare? She loved him so much she couldn't bear the thought of leaving. She knew she had made the right decision in staying here with him no matter what her family said. Being with this man in this place was the right thing, the only thing, for her to do. They would be together to the very end. Nothing could change that.

He was leaning over her, adjusting her pillow to make sure she was as comfortable as she could be. "Are the kids here?" she asked.

His expression betrayed a hint of despair. "I've called them. They'll be here soon."

"They'll be mad if I leave before they arrive."

"So I guess you better stick around." He tried to smile but felt certain the look on his face did nothing to provide her any reassurance.

Running out of things to do that would justify his presence in the room, he finally sat in the old rocking chair next to the bed. He wanted to say so much, express how much he loved her, how grateful he was that she stayed when everyone told her she shouldn't, how sorry he was about the whole rotten situation. But he just sat in silence as they steadily gazed into each other's eyes, everything that needed to be said being communicated without words. She knew how he felt. He knew how she felt. After so many years together, after going through so much, the words didn't need to be spoken.

After a while, she broke the beautiful silence. "I want to see the decorations." She had a desire to move, feeling if she lay there any longer she might die then and there in that bed. She started to prop herself up as much as she could. "Are they all up?"

Brought out of his thoughts by her question, he leaned forward in the chair. "I haven't done as much as you normally do but there is still time. I can never do it as good as you anyway."

She gave him a look. *Her* look. The look he had seen a thousand times. She never liked it when he made himself seem incapable. He had accomplished so much in his life and she simply didn't tolerate hearing him speak like he couldn't do something. As far as she was concerned, he could do anything he set his mind to and she had never seen him not accomplish whatever goals he set for himself. But she also knew he would often dismiss his own abilities to make her feel like she could do some things better than him. Decorating for Christmas was one of those things she excelled at but she knew he was better at it than most men. "Can I see?"

With a sly, wide grin, he quickly got up from the chair and moved to the bed. "I thought you'd never ask!" He carefully lifted her and placed her into the wheelchair sitting in the corner. He situated her feet on the foot rests and lifted her favorite red tartan blanket from the foot of the bed to cover her legs. "Comfortable?"

She couldn't help but wince a bit as he set her in the chair, hoping he didn't notice. Him moving

her hurt more than he could possibly understand but she couldn't let him know. After all, it wasn't his fault. "That's great. Thanks."

He wheeled her down the hallway into the wide and spacious great room of their house, then maneuvered her around so she could view all the decorations. She was pleased to see he had adorned the grand stone fireplace mantle with a fresh white pine garland that had twinkling soft white lights woven throughout. Then, she was happy to see he had used the new gold ribbon she bought on their last trip together, right before she started to feel sick. With everything that was going on with her illness, she had forgotten to use it the previous year. But now it reminded her of a much happier time and was thankful to see it used as intended, impressed at how he expertly wove it through the garland that outlined the entrance to the dining area. The window sills were decorated with festive greens and flickering candle lights as was their tradition. She smiled as she saw that he remembered some of her special touches, placing little items like snowmen and church mice figures in corners and on ledges scattered around the room. She loved putting things in unlikely places so when they entertained people would see something festive no matter where they were in the house. But this year it seemed unlikely any entertaining would happen.

"It's all beautiful. You did a wonderful job."

"You aren't going to give me a hard time about the skiing Santa this year?" He knew she was not a fan of his favorite decoration, a foot tall Santa figure holding skis. It was a bit kitschy but he immediately liked it when he came upon it in a store years ago and bought it without thinking what she might say. And every year when he brought it out, she would act exasperated and exclaim 'you're not putting that out again?!?' He was never really certain if she hated it or just liked giving him static about it as a holiday tradition. Either way, he put it out every year. It reminded him of fun times with his family, times that were now distant memories. But they were still good memories.

She gave a very slight smile and shook her head. "I just don't have the energy. You like it, although I can't imagine why, but that's all that matters." She gave a weak wave of her hand. "Enjoy."

"I will." He smiled slightly to mask his concern regarding her statement that she didn't have energy. To most, that would just be a figure of speech. But in her case, it meant she was fading.

"I wish I could go on the tree hunt this year but I just can't. Do you have your eye on one in particular?"

"I've been trimming up a few for the past couple years that should be ready by now."

"Get one that fills up the whole corner." It was tradition to place their tree in the large, spacious corner next to the fireplace. When searching for the right tree some years, they would be worried the tree they had picked would be too big for the space. But so far, they had never cut one that didn't fit the large area. "You know how I love a nice, full tree."

"I do. And I'm certain I can find one that will fulfill your expectations!"

"And don't forget to hang the wreaths on the gates. Did you remember to order them?" she asked anxiously.

"They'll be here in a few days. Don't worry, I'll have them in place in plenty of time."

He leaned on the handles of her chair as they spoke, not sure if he should take her back to bed or let her remain in the room, surrounded by the festivity she loved so much. Her spirits seemed to be lifted by seeing her favorite decorations all properly placed so he figured they should stay there as long as she wanted. *What good would being in bed do at this point?*

She suddenly got a chill. "I'm cold."

He maneuvered her chair nearer the fireplace, then thought it would be better to lift her up and sit in his favorite chair with her in his lap. It was the chair they would snuggle in on movie night when the kids were young, knowing it would cause their son and daughter great embarrassment at seeing their parent's display of affection. He smiled at the memory as she settled into his lap. She had lost so much weight the experience didn't feel the same. But then, nothing was like it used to be. For now, he was glad to have her so close. He made sure the blanket was covering as much of her as possible and as she felt the warmth of his body against hers, she started to relax. They watched the fire dancing in the fireplace, their hearts beating in steady rhythm as the crackling fire warmed them both. Sitting and watching the fire had been a favorite pastime, when time allowed, which hadn't been often enough in the past. Their lives had been so busy they often forgot to take time to relax. They knew they weren't unique. Most people never took time to relax and appreciate the gifts they had been given. Life was too hectic. But now all they could do was relax. She had been mostly bedridden in recent weeks so he was thankful she had wanted to get out of their room for a change of scenery at her favorite time of year. He prayed it would help.

Her deep blue eyes felt heavy and as the fire warmed her, she eventually closed them, enjoying being as close to her husband as she possibly could.

He held her tightly, wishing the moment would never end, praying for a miracle he knew wasn't

coming, reflecting on their lifetime of wonderful memories and on a lifetime that was too short.

Then after a while, she left....before the kids arrived.

CHAPTER 1

Sue Stevens was in a rut! And she knew it. But did her followers know it? After all, they deserved better than rehashes of the same story, year after year. Had they noticed she hadn't really been doing anything new over the last few Christmases? She hoped not. But she knew she had to do something different, something better, before it was too late. It took her years to build her reputation as one of the best travel writers in the industry, someone her devoted readers could depend on to provide vital information. They followed everything she wrote and planned vacations, weddings, honeymoons, family reunions and more to the places she described so perfectly in her magazine articles and on her blog. People in the places she visited told her how she perfectly captured the charm of their towns and over the years her fans often said her style of vividly describing the places she found made them want to visit the out-of-the-way gems she discovered. She had built a career and a life out of her love of travel and discovery. And she wasn't about to lose it all. But if she didn't come up with something different for her annual Christmas article, she felt certain people might start to see she had lost her zeal. She wasn't sure when it happened, but she didn't seem to have the same zest for discovering new and different places and ways to celebrate the holiday. She really wasn't getting much satisfaction from her work anymore. *What has happened to me?* she asked herself much too often lately.

She thought back to how it all started. As a little girl, Christmas was her favorite time of year. The beauty of the decorations, the excitement of what Santa might bring, the delicious baked treats and the places her family visited each year all combined to make Christmas a most wondrous time of the year for Sue. And her parents had taught her about the wonder of travel early in life, setting the tone for a career that had taken her to so many places she never could have imagined in her youth.

Sue was five years old when her parents decided to rent a cabin in the mountains for their Christmas celebration that year. A Christmas Eve snowfall created the picture-perfect "Hallmark setting" for their holiday. However, Sue was worried Santa wouldn't be able to find her at the cabin deep in the woods so her parents found clever ways to make the holiday special so she wouldn't worry. They strung popcorn on Christmas Eve to decorate the tree outside their cabin door. They baked cookies just for Santa and placed them by the tree. Her father did a perfect reading of "'Twas The Night Before Christmas" by the roaring fire. With so much to do, Sue forgot her fear of Santa not finding her, which was totally put to rest Christmas morning when presents were found under the tree, just as her parents had promised. His reindeer even ate the popcorn they had strung on the tree outside! *Santa truly was magical* Sue thought as her father started a fire to warm the room while her mother made hot chocolate. And after opening presents, they had Christmas cookies for breakfast! She thought it was the best Christmas ever...until the next one, and the one after that and the one after that. Every year, her parents found a different place and a different way to celebrate the holiday, which always made it a magical time of year. Yes, Christmas was Sue's favorite holiday. Which was why her annual Christmas article was the cornerstone of her work. Her fans came to depend on her delivering an article every year that would not only make them want to visit the place Sue had found but also inspire their own holiday traditions. Every year she managed to find unique places to explore.

*****

Sue's life had been a series of twists and turns. Her parents instilled a love of travel and discovery in her that had served her well as an adult. A youth full of wonderful holiday celebrations and fun family vacations to all manner of places was not to be taken for granted. After all, they formed the foundation of Sue's career. And she was eternally grateful for this as well as her parents support for her love of animals. They always found room for the strays she would bring home as long as she took good care of them and recognized the responsibility of properly caring for an animal. Her pets had quickly become her best friends and she never wanted to let them down. These days she missed having an animal in her life since the traveling she did for work didn't allow for a pet.

But overall, Sue was satisfied with where she was in life. Except in regard to her parents. They were so close in her formative years that she had been looking forward to being able to depend on their wisdom and advice as an adult. Sometimes, she still had trouble comprehending why they were no longer in her life except through the wonderful memories she treasured. Kids are supposed to be able to depend on their parents...always. But when hers were senselessly killed while Sue was in college, she was so devastated she almost dropped out. *What was the point of college?* She turned the thought over and over in her head until it hurt. Then she considered changing her major to law so she could work to keep criminals behind bars in honor of her parent's memory. But she thought of how disappointing it would be to them if she gave up studying something she loved so much. In the end, she stuck with journalism and obtained her degree. The thought of how proud her parents would be if they were sitting in the auditorium during her graduation ceremony carried her through.

The one thing Sue did change about her planned future was move to the city from her childhood home in upstate New York. She never planned to venture too far from her roots but devastation can make plans change. She knew that a change of surroundings would do wonders for her mentally and with the city being so hectic, she figured she wouldn't have time to ponder what could have, should have been.

Shortly after college, she started writing a travel blog. Through hustle and determination she landed in her current situation writing for the top travel magazine, her articles published in five languages for editions sold in Europe and South America. She was also was the top blogger on the magazine's website, her blog entries consistently viewed by her multitude of dedicated followers. She was fortunate in that her vocation allowed indulgence in her love of travel and writing.

Her living conditions were not what she had planned however. Her apartment was small, too small for anything more than a loveseat, a small dining table and a comfy leather chair she could sink into for a night of movie-watching when time allowed. She did manage to squeeze a large desk into one corner of her abode so she could spread out her notes when writing so she didn't miss a detail she wanted to include in her articles. But the cramped space meant she couldn't have anything more than a table-top Christmas tree to decorate her space for the holidays. She told herself that she really didn't need more space. More space meant more stuff, which she most likely didn't actually need. She was on-the-road most of the time anyway. She had what she needed. Life was good.

Or was it? Something hadn't felt quite right lately and Sue didn't know why. She had accomplished so much and ended up with her dream job which combined two of the three things that had consumed her youth. She knew that traveling and writing about those travels was what she wanted to do. But lately she felt an urge, a drive, for something different. What that something different was, she wasn't sure. And she found herself being easily irritated recently. The smallest, inconsequential thing could set her off. *Why?* It was very unlike her. And while it was true she didn't have anyone special in her life, she had close friends who were in a similar situation. They all made a pact to not worry about finding a special someone. If they were meant to be with someone, they would know it when that person came along. They all firmly believed this. So Sue was sure that wasn't what was affecting her mood of late or her need for change. But she knew that change was indeed what she needed. And her annual Christmas article seemed to be the best place to start!

For years, it had been Sue's tradition to find a quaint town to explore and then write about their traditions and the charming ways in which they celebrated Christmas. But for some time now, it seemed to her that she was basically discovering the same small town over and over. After years of celebrating the holiday in various parts of the country and Europe, it seemed to her as though they had all run together to make one big blur, with no distinction from one to the other. *This year would be different!*

Even in years when Sue didn't have trouble getting inspiration for her writing, she would have trouble getting into the mood to do the research. After all, in October, people are getting ready for Halloween, not Christmas, although it was hard to tell in recent years. It annoyed her that it was considered normal for Halloween and Christmas decorations to be displayed side by side at stores these days. *Can't we get one holiday over with before they start shoving the next one down everyone's throats?*

She sat in her "home office" and opened her computer. Her process for writing the article was the same every year. First, she needed to set the mood. To that end, she opened her Christmas music playlist. She had always loved Christmas music and several years prior had put together an eclectic mix of songs that she enjoyed from Thanksgiving through Christmas every year. The playlist contained songs that reminded her of the Christmases of her youth, favorite versions of classic songs introduced to her by her parents and newer favorites she had discovered over the years since college. She loved every one of the hundreds of songs she had put together, even though her friends sometimes shook their heads when they were celebrating together and something less than traditional played. She didn't care. Christmas music was her favorite. She clicked on shuffle and smiled as the music began to play.

A search for Christmas images got Sue's research started as she scrolled through pictures of holiday celebrations. She viewed picture after picture of people baking cookies, decorating trees, sitting before a roaring fire under a mantle festively adorned with greens and lights. There were pictures of carolers singing for elderly people in nursing homes, kids sitting on Santa's lap, beautifully decorated Christmas cookies and nurses decorating hospital corridors to help brighten their patient's spirits. There were pictures of firemen receiving the gift of a Dalmatian puppy with a big red bow around its neck and of a soup kitchen handing out delicious looking meals to people who had little to celebrate but did so anyway. She found images of postal workers sorting letters to Santa, making sure they were forwarded to charities that might help make a Christmas wish come true for a deserving child. There were pictures of school children in plays and holiday parties and festive decorations. Picture-perfect villages nestled in snow-covered mountains and images of palm trees on a tropical beach decorated with colored lights. Picture after non-inspiring picture scrolled by as Sue started to feel she would never find what she needed. Then she found it! A single picture that provided her with much needed inspiration! She stopped scrolling as her screen filled with the image of a snow-covered field. Slightly off center of the scene, a cowboy was leaning on a fence decorated with a simple green wreath. He was looking directly into the camera lens with such a peaceful expression that it instantly made Sue want to examine the photo further.

She stared for several moments at the calm, reassuring face staring back at her. The picture made her think back to her youth. Had things been different, she might have easily been in that picture, staring at the camera. Lost in thoughts long forgotten, she wondered how the person she was staring at celebrated the birth of Jesus. All the pictures she had scrolled through represented how so many people celebrated the blessed holiday and she could have easily filled in the narrative behind the images of people decorating ginger bread houses or discovering a puppy under the tree. But she had no thoughts behind the holiday traditions of a cowboy. She had always looked at cowboys as being rugged, tough men and women who might not have given a thought to the traditions of Christmas. But this man looked peaceful, happy, excited and tired all at the same time. Tired was easy to understand. Being a cowboy was tough work. But she couldn't quite figure out the other emotions she felt from this picture. *What do cowboys do at Christmas?*

This was the inspiration she desperately needed! Instead of examining and describing how a small town celebrated, she would look at how people with non-traditional occupations celebrate the holiday. Doctors and nurses, firemen and nursing home staff, prison guards and police, anyone she could think of that didn't work a traditional 9 to 5 job. But cowboys would be her main focus. Did cowboys have certain holiday traditions that would be foreign to most people, something they might not even understand? Did they do things some people might think of as odd or not celebratory at all? Her head was starting to reel with the questions she wanted answered! But she was getting ahead of herself. The cowboy portion of her holiday writing would have to wait. Her annual Christmas article always came in two parts. The first part was printed in the magazine at the beginning of December. And the second part, the main focus, was always put on the magazine's website a few days before Christmas. So this year, the printed article would be about doctors and police, etc. The website portion would be about cowboys.

Sue's excitement grew as she prepared to put her story together. She thought it would be a surprise to her readers but one she hoped they would accept. She needed to be thorough in her research though, if she expected her readers to embrace what she was doing. With 3 weeks to research and write the first part, she felt she had enough time. But she had to get started!

*****

Sue looked up from her screen to check the time. 2:00 am! Suddenly, she realized how tired she was. Several hours of research led to phone calls which resulted in on-the-spot interviews as well as appointments for in-person interviews. Then she had started writing an outline along with snippets of thoughts she wanted to be certain to insert into the final printed article. Now, at 2:00 am, she felt satisfied with what she had accomplished. With Christmas music still filling the room, she looked over what she had written. As she saved her work and was about to turn off the music, a song started to play that stopped her actions. It was a favorite song she discovered on a Christmas album in her parents record collection long ago. And how appropriate it was for John Denver's "Christmas For Cowboys" to start playing at that moment! The song described the personal, quiet Christmas celebrations of cowboys as they appreciated the gift of a wide open plain and a campfire for warmth along with the feeling of contentment they experienced during the holiday. How many of the traditions mentioned in the lyrics would turn out to be real? Sue listened to the entire song. It brought back so many childhood memories. Holiday celebrations, horseback riding and much more. Memories long forgotten that were now flooding back to her, confirming that this year's article was going to be special.

CHAPTER 2

The magazine's offices were starting to look and feel festive. With Thanksgiving a few days away, everyone was cheerful and several people had started to decorate their desk areas for Christmas. It was an unwritten rule that Christmas décor couldn't make its way into the office space until after turkey day but there were always a few that pushed the limits. Sue found herself a bit irritated by the stretching of the rule this year. She wasn't sure why. She usually loved it when Christmas decorations started to pop up at the office but this year, it just bugged her. However, she was trying not to dwell on it. She had put the finishing touches on her print article and was satisfied with the results. More importantly, her editor was satisfied. Steve thought the idea was fresh and since he had been gently nudging Sue to change things up without being obnoxious about it, he was pleased she realized that change was needed so he didn't have to *tell* her it was needed. She liked a lot of things about her editor, but his style of not pressuring her was what she appreciated the most.

Before Sue submitted her article to the print department, she wandered into the break room to calm down. She had just snapped at her assistant for something that was important but not vital. She immediately apologized but realized that the whole brief incident was very out of character. *Why am I so wound up lately?* she asked herself. Lost in her self-examining thoughts while staring at her coffee, she looked up to see Mark, the newest addition to the staff, walking in. She quickly shifted her train of thought. She hadn't really had the opportunity to talk to him since his arrival as she had been busy with the article and he had only been there a few weeks. *Perfect chance to get to know the newbie!*

"Hey Mark. Sue Stevens." She stood and put out her hand to shake his. "We met on your first day and haven't had a chance to chat since, which is my fault. Too immersed in work."

"Hi Sue. I do seem to remember you flashing by me during my first week."

The wry smile on Mark's face told her he had a sense of humor. *We're going to get along just fine.* "How are you liking it here?"

"So far, so good. I'm learning how things work, what needs to be done, the ins and outs of who to avoid."

Sue gave a knowing nod. "You've met Yvonne. She loves new blood. Can't think of anyone she hasn't hit on. And she will steal a story idea faster than you can get it out of your mouth so keep them to yourself when she's around"

"Thanks for the advice."

"I read your article on the updated vaccines needed for travel to the Far East. Nice work."

"You must have been having trouble getting to sleep one night if you made it through that piece," Mark laughed. "It's a pretty dry subject but people need the information. Hopefully I'll be writing more intriguing stuff soon."

"You'll find your niche." Sue decided she liked Mark. He seemed level headed, which was a very attractive feature to Sue. But his trim figure and obvious attention to grooming showed he took good care of himself. His light brown hair was short and neat and for the first time, she noticed his hazel eyes. He had an air of sophistication that suggested he did not grow up locally but was perhaps more well-traveled. If he was older, Yvonne might have some competition for his attention. If Sue was in the mood for such things. These days, she didn't seem to be in the mood for much of anything. *Why?* Before she allowed her mood to turn sour again, she decided she wanted to know more about the new guy. "So I assume you're excited to go home for the holiday."

He turned slightly somber as he spoke hesitantly. "Not really planning to go anywhere."

Sue was caught off-guard by his sudden change in demeanor. *There's a story there.* "No plans for heading to Grandma's house for turkey and stuffing?" Her attempt to lighten the mood worked, a little.

"No over the river and through the woods for me this year. Figure I'll stay in the city and relax with some takeout."

Sue surprised herself when she suddenly turned forward and forceful. "Nope, that won't do. My best friend throws a Friendsgiving dinner every year for our friends who can't get home to be with family for the holiday. This year you are coming as my guest." The thought of Mark being alone in a new city on a holiday made for family and friends suddenly brought out a maternal instinct in her. And she didn't know why.

"Thanks but that's really not necessary."

"Don't be silly." She sensed he was interested but hesitant. "Unlock your phone and give it to me."

Mark did as instructed, not sure exactly what was happening. Sue took the phone and typed in it for several moments, then handed it back.

"That's the address. Meet me there at five o'clock sharp."

"Sue, I really appreciate it but I don't want to impose."

"You aren't imposing. This dinner is literally made for people like us. Besides, you're new in town and you need to meet people outside of this office."

"Shouldn't you check with your friend first?"

"Believe me, Melanie would be very upset if I didn't invite you! Just bring her a nice Pinot Noir and she'll be your friend for life."

"Really, I..."

Before he could get another word out, she put up her hand to stop him and spoke a bit more gently. "Please, I really would like for you to be there." Then a mischievous smile came across her face. "And if you don't show, I'll tell Yvonne you've been interested in her since the day you first met!"

The expression of mock horror that came across Mark's face told Sue he was worth getting to know better. She was looking forward to taking him to Melanie's Friendsgiving feast. "See you Thursday. Five o'clock sharp!"

CHAPTER 3

Sue and Melanie met in college, two freshmen thrown together by student housing. People who didn't know them well always assumed there must be a rivalry between them since both were beauties who often attracted the attention of the same men. It seemed to most that Sue's striking features along with her blue eyes and Melanie's long legs and slender figure couldn't possibly co-exist without jealousy ensuing. But the two got along famously from the start. To both of them, it seemed as though they had known each other their whole lives. And when Sue's parents were suddenly gone, she realized just how strong their friendship was. Melanie instinctively knew what to do to help comfort her friend. Sue felt she never would have stayed in school or stuck with her chosen field if it hadn't been for Melanie. With both of them studying journalism, one in writing and the other in photography, they made a pact to work together once they graduated and the desire to do just that helped Sue stay on course. After the two friends graduated, they went back to their respective homes but spoke to each other multiple times each day. When Sue eventually got a starting position at the top travel magazine, she finagled an interview for Melanie, which led to her becoming a freelance photographer for the publication. And they soon found themselves living together again, this time in a comfortable 2 bedroom apartment in the Philadelphia suburbs, not far from the magazine's offices. Since they were close to New York, it wasn't long before Melanie was freelancing as a photographer and doing quite well while Sue steadily built her career.

During the process of moving into their new abode, Sue and Melanie met their neighbor Jackie, who was younger and, at first, seemingly a bit wild. She was constantly having friends over for parties and always invited her new neighbors. Sue and Melanie didn't join in Jackie's more wild gatherings but it didn't take long for them to realize their new friend was masking loneliness. One night over several bottles of wine, the three shared intimate details of their pasts as only close friends do. Jackie revealed that her parents deserted her in her youth and she had been passed around from relative to relative. In every living situation she had known, she knew it could end at any moment and she lived in constant fear of being left alone. Once she was finally old enough to live on her own, her party days started in earnest. Her beauty and trim figure, which were accented by her knack for choosing clothing that accentuated her best assets perfectly, attracted a great deal of attention, which she was all too willing oblige. Until one night things almost got out of hand. The details were unimportant. What was important is that the incident woke her up to the fact that she needed to slow down and get herself together before it was too late. She had seen more than one of the friends of her youth get into trouble in one way or another and she was sensible enough to know she could not to let it happen to her. While she still enjoyed dating as much as possible, she was now much more careful as to the company she kept and counted on Sue and Melanie to keep her in line, which they were happy to do. When the three of them would go out together, their credo was 'men of the world beware'! Everywhere they went the beauty of blonde Sue, brunette Melanie and redhead Jackie attracted admiring stares and plenty of innocent and some not-so-innocent conversation. But if they weren't in the mood for anyone to interrupt their evening out, they stuck together in shutting down the unwanted advances with class and finesse.

Nowadays, years after each of them had moved out of the building where they first met, they were as close as ever and spent as much time together as their busy careers would allow. They gathered for holiday celebrations as often as possible with Melanie's Friendsgiving dinner being Sue's favorite. The party had been a tradition for years. With no family of her own to celebrate with, Melanie looked forward to making sure her friends enjoyed a traditional holiday feast together, knowing that friends could be as good as family, sometimes better. Every year the mix of people changed a bit, based on who was able to get home for the holiday. But Melanie could always count on Sue and Jackie to be there. Which was a good thing since, as the celebration grew each year, Melanie needed help getting everything prepared.

Sue surveyed the spacious condo. Even though it was more room than needed, she was certain Melanie chose it so she could host large gatherings. She loved entertaining and it showed in how she decorated for each party, paying attention to the smallest of details, while making friends old and new feel welcome in her home. Grey and white were the basic colors of the walls and trim but Melanie managed to introduce color in unique ways. While most people would use colorful pillows as accents, she chose to use vases, decorative plates and bowls along with tasteful paintings to add texture, warmth, and color to the space. Area rugs were strategically placed sparingly, since the floors were made of beautiful reclaimed wood with gray and brown tones. For the Thanksgiving holiday, Sue noted a large wreath made of interwoven dried twigs and pinecones with natural dried leaves of a deep yellow color placed sporadically throughout hanging over the fireplace along with several clusters of small decorative pumpkins around the living and dining areas. In the center of Melanie's large dining table was a centerpiece made up of gourds, dried leaves, pumpkins and turkey feathers. Candles with a soft scent of spice glowed throughout the space, their scent mixing beautifully with the appetizing odors wafting from the kitchen.

"Melanie, your place looks absolutely perfect!" Sue exclaimed as she took in everything there was to see. "I don't know how you manage to make it look so different for every gathering."

"It helps when your best friend happens to be a renowned traveler who writes detailed articles about the places she visits and the celebrations she experiences."

Ever the jokester, Jackie interrupted. "But I'm not a renowned traveler!"

The three looked at each other and giggled before Melanie continued. "It's easy for me to get new inspiration for every holiday. I just recreate what you describe."

"Well thank you for the compliment but I think this all comes from your creativity," Sue stated matter-of-factly. "I doubt I have anything at all to do with it!"

Sue and Jackie had been at Melanie's condo all afternoon and the place was starting to smell like a proper turkey dinner was just about ready as the guests arrived. Everyone was welcomed to the celebration by an excited Melanie and her latest holiday cocktail creation; warm cider mulled with cinnamon sticks and cloves, a few secret spices and dry red wine added just before serving. The reaction of each guest told Melanie her creation was a success. And the odors coming from the kitchen told everyone a sumptuous meal was in store for them as they tried not to fill up on a selection of hors d'oeuvres that were too good to resist, knowing they would regret over-indulging when the real meal was served.

A jazz trio recording by pianist Marian McPartland played softly in the background as guests caught up on each other's lives as some hadn't seen each other since the previous year's celebration. Everyone was so busy, there never seemed to be enough time to slow down and enjoy being with friends.

This year there was only one new face among the guests. "Mark, I'm so glad you made it!" Sue exclaimed as he arrived.

"Thanks very much for the invitation," he replied. "After your description of the event, I couldn't resist experiencing it for myself."

"I'm glad you were intrigued enough to join us. I don't think you'll be disappointed." She wondered why such an amiable young man didn't have anywhere to go for the holiday.

As Sue spoke, Melanie glided up beside her, putting out her hand. "Hi, I'm Melanie. You must be Mark. I've heard quite a bit about you!"

As they shook hands, Jackie suddenly appeared next to Sue. Eyeing Mark up and down, she gave an approving smile as she also shook his hand. "I'm Jackie. And I'm certain I haven't heard enough about you!" The gleam in her eye was about to turn lustful when Melanie brought her back to reality.

"Down girl. At least let the man get a drink before you pounce!" She turned to Mark as she continued. "Come with me. You need to get caught up on your libation consumption."

"Speaking of which." Mark looked down at the bottle of red wine in his hand as he held it out for Melanie. "This is for you. Thank you for having me."

As she accepted the bottle, she gave a very approving nod. "My favorite vintage. Thank you very much."

"Sue helped with the selection. She mentioned you like this particular one."

"Ahh, it's wonderful having friends who know me so well," she responded with a slight giggle. "Come on, let's get you a drink and I'll open this so it can breathe." She playfully hooked her arm through his and led the way to the kitchen. After Mark had a mug of warm cider in his hand, she introduced him to some of the guests then excused herself to make the final dinner preparations.

Excitement ensued in the kitchen as casseroles were removed from the oven, the golden brown turkey was carved, potatoes were mashed and gravy was stirred. The feast was coming together nicely as Sue surveyed all of the food. "Melanie, everything looks so delicious. I don't know how you do it."

"It's really not that tough. Everyone brings so many wonderful dishes each year all I have to do is stuff the bird with my mother's secret stuffing recipe and pop it in the oven for a few hours. Then it's just a matter of plating everything and putting it on the buffet."

"You're too modest. You do more than just cook a turkey and you do a fabulous job of putting it all together every year!" Jackie exclaimed. "And one of these year's I'm going to get your mother's stuffing recipe!"

*****

As the last spaces on her buffet were filled with delectable delights, Melanie gave everything the "once-over". One year she had forgotten to put out her famous cranberry salad and while everyone missed it, no one had the courage to say anything. When she found it in the back of her fridge while putting away leftovers, all she could do was laugh out loud at her forgetfulness, vowing to never let it happen again! Looking over everything as she ticked off the list running through her head, she was satisfied nothing had been forgotten. So with everything in its proper place, she turned to her guests and proudly proclaimed, "Dinner is served."

Everyone quickly gathered in the dining area, knowing what was awaiting their eager palettes. Even though Melanie's dining table was larger than normal, it wasn't big enough to seat everyone so she had placed small tables around the condo for guests to sit in smaller groups and continue their conversations over dinner. But before anyone dug into the food, there was a tradition to be followed. It started when Melanie was a child and she carried it through to her Friendsgiving celebrations.

"Before we start, please get a drink and join me in a toast." As everyone grabbed their drinks, Sue made her way over to Mark, who seemed to be getting to know the other guests well on his own. But since she had been busy helping with meal preparation, she didn't want him to feel neglected during the toast.

With everyone holding their beverage of choice, Melanie began. "Even though it's been a bit of a tough year in some ways, we all have things for which we can be thankful on this day. Like Monica's new promotion, Mike's cancer being in remission, Tom's mother being out of the hospital and Darlene's son being stationed in a relatively safe post overseas. It's easy to find negative things to dwell on but I'm pretty sure we all have more positive things going on in our lives than we often realize. So tonight let's be thankful for our health, our comfortable livings, our friendships and all of the good things in our lives, both big and small." Melanie looked around at everyone gathered together and raised her glass. "Happy Thanksgiving everyone. Thank you for being here!"

Glasses clinked together as everyone responded with a robust "Happy Thanksgiving"!

"OK," Melanie exclaimed. "Dig in. And don't be shy. There is plenty of food!"

Guests patiently worked their way through the buffet line and filled their plates with juicy turkey, stuffing and casseroles of sweet potatoes, corn pudding, green beans and more. And no one passed on Melanie's cranberry salad! As everyone found places to sit, either at the dining table or around the living area and in the kitchen, conversations continued or started anew as they enjoyed the delicious food. Multiple compliments on the meal were given as most went back for seconds.

As everyone finished their meals, Melanie could see they all had their fill but there was still a mountain of food on her buffet. She smiled to herself. *One year I'll make just the right amount.* But this was not the year.

And while just about everyone groaned and patted their full stomachs while proclaiming they 'couldn't eat another bite', when Jackie's fresh pumpkin and Jen's chocolate chip pecan pies were brought out, everyone ate another bite!

With dessert complete, Melanie was satisfied that another successful Friendsgiving meal had been thoroughly enjoyed. Several guests helped with washing casserole dishes while others helped put away leftovers, much of which was packed into to-go bags. Melanie was determined not have the dinner in her refrigerator for a week!

With cleanup accomplished, Sue, Melanie and Jackie each got a drink and sat down together, the first time all evening they had some real time to talk.

Jackie looked at Mark across the room as he was talking with one of their friends. Then she smiled at Sue. "So, you and Mark. Anything happening there?"

Sue looked at her like she had three heads. "Don't you think he's a bit young for me?"

"Yes, but I wanted you to say it!" She laughed as she eyed him across the room. "You have to admit though, he's cute."

"Well, I don't disagree. But he's closer to your age than mine". She knew Mark was Jackie's type which was one of the reasons she invited him.

Melanie gave Sue a knowing look as she spoke in a slightly teasing tone. "Jackie, maybe you can see what he's doing for New Year's Eve."

She smiled. "Not a bad idea. It's been a while since I brought in the New Year with a bang!" They looked at each other and burst into laughter, which they quickly downgraded to a giggle so no one would ask them what was so funny.

Melanie brought the conversation back to reality. "OK, serious question Sue. How is the annual Christmas celebration article coming?"

A concerned expression came over Sue's face. "Slow."

This was a surprise! "What?? You're usually almost finished by now. What happened?"

"I feel like I've been in a rut lately and it took me a while to figure out how to freshen up my Christmas article."

Jackie was puzzled. "What do you mean 'freshen it up'? Every year you find some quaint little town and perfectly describe their holiday traditions in amazing detail. That's what your readers look forward to each year. You don't need to freshen anything up!"

"Yes I do. I just feel like I'm describing the same thing over and over. There are only so many ways to celebrate in these small towns. I read my last three Christmas articles and I honestly couldn't differentiate between each of the towns I wrote about. They literally all ran together in my head."

"So what did you decide to do?" Melanie inquired hesitantly. "I'm not sure your readers are ready for too drastic of a change."

"I decided that instead of describing one celebration in one town, I'd write about how people in non-traditional jobs celebrate the holiday, show what people do who don't work 9 to 5."

Melanie and Jackie both gave her a look of confusion. "Examples please," Melanie demanded.

Sue hesitated, wanting to make sure she gave her friends a good example of what she was trying to accomplish. "Truck drivers. They are on the road all through the holiday season, getting products where they need to be, fulfilling our needs daily. After all, it's not Santa who gets those on-line orders to your door the next day. And while these people may not be able to go to holiday parties and enjoy some of the traditions that most of us take for granted, I figured they still have their own holiday traditions that they look forward to each year."

Jackie considered the idea for a moment. "I guess I never thought about it that way."

"Exactly. Most people don't. But think about doctors and nurses, firemen and police, air traffic controllers and pilots. All of them are working on Christmas. There are emergency utility workers everywhere who are on call constantly and regardless of the time, day…or holiday, when they are needed they are prepared to go to work. Did you know that December 8th is National Blue Collar Workers Recognition Day? I didn't. These people need to be appreciated and I want to help them get some recognition with my article this year while exploring what they do at Christmas."

Melanie and Jackie both shook their heads as they tried to fully comprehend their friend's idea.

"My thought was that all of these professions have traditions that are similar within their fields regardless of where they live. For example, I found that police as a group often do something to help charity organizations at Christmas, most choosing to help women and children who are trying to avoid abusive situations. And nurses tend to do something to help brighten the holiday for families of kids who are undergoing long term treatment. But to be honest, I was hoping I'd find more unique similarities between more professions." Sue shrugged her shoulders. "Fortunately, I was able to find enough to put together the print article coming out Monday so I think it worked."

"Sounds intriguing, but what about the blog? That's the main thing people look forward to each year."

"I know." Concern was evident in her expression. "That's where I've fallen behind. I know what I want to write about but I'm having trouble lining up people to interview."

"Well don't keep us in suspense." Melanie coaxed. "What's the focus of your feature?"

Sue hesitated for a few moments, hoping her friends wouldn't be too disappointed. "Cowboys."

"Cowboys?!? How did you come up with that?" Jackie tried to sound supportive but couldn't fathom why her friend had picked her chosen subject.

"It goes back to when I was a little girl. Not sure why but I always fanaticized that a cowboy would ride up one day and carry me away."

Jackie raised her eyebrows. "Not a bad fantasy at all!"

"Steady girl." Melanie wasn't surprised at all by her friend's reaction. She was constantly searching for new men in her life. *She needs to settle down with the right guy!* Turning to Sue, she inquired further. "So tell us why you want to write about how a cowboy celebrates Christmas."

"I've always been fascinated with cowboys and how they live. I love watching movies and reading books about them and now something has motivated me to write about their holiday traditions. The life of a cowboy has always seemed romantic to me, in a rugged way. But they basically work all the time, regardless of the day... or holiday. I'm thinking they probably have some very nice holiday traditions that involve campfires and warm blankets and sleeping under the stars."

"Well, that's certainly *un-traditional* for you," Melanie mused.

"Before you scoff too much, just remember that if it weren't for cowboys, you wouldn't enjoy your traditional prime rib dinner every Christmas!"

Melanie feigned horror. "Bite your tongue!" Then shock came over her. "OMG, this means my next year's holiday decorations are going to be inspired by hay and horses and manure. I know Jesus was born in a stable but I don't know if I can even find a manure scented candle!" They giggled at Melanie's preposterous dilemma.

"I don't know." Jackie mused thoughtfully. "The idea of a hot cowboy in leather chaps serving me Christmas dinner is definitely appealing!" Before anyone could say anything, she shook herself from her fantasy world. "So how is the research coming?"

"A bit frustrating. There's only so much I can accomplish sitting at my computer. I've been trying to find some real cowboys or cowgirls to interview but everyone I've contacted seems hesitant to talk to me."

"That's because they think you're putting them on." Mark had been standing near the three woman, taking note of their conversation and finally interjected as he heard mention of cowboys. "Pretty sure they don't think anyone is interested in their holiday traditions."

Sue was surprised by his statement. "You speak as though you're an expert on them."

He held up his hands in surrender. "Definitely not an expert. But I used to know a few. Probably the best thing to do is go out to a ranch and talk to them in person, let them see you're sincere."

"I'd love to but I'm not sure where to start." Sue couldn't help but think he wasn't saying as much as he could on the subject. "Got any suggestions?"

"Montana has some of the biggest cattle ranches in the county." As an afterthought, he continued with a barely noticeable hint of regret. "I used to know someone who had one there."

Sue perked up at the prospect of making progress in her research. "Great! Can you connect me with them?"

His demeanor darkened a bit more. "Sorry, we lost touch. But you should be able to find someone out there that'll talk to you about how cowboys celebrate the holiday, if they celebrate it at all." Suddenly his voice became harsh and judgmental. "Mostly I've found them to be cold, hard people. Probably because of what they do for a living. Not a life for the weak. It's a tough and basic existence."

Sue, Melanie and Jackie exchanged looks of *whoa, what's this all about?* Sue eventually acknowledged his comments with a smile. "Thanks, I'll look into Montana ranches tomorrow and see what I can line up."

With a far-away look in his eyes, Mark turned while mumbling something about needing another drink and meandered away, seeming to regret that he had joined in on the conversation. Jackie followed him, whispering something in his ear that seemed to bring him back to being himself, at least the self that Sue saw around the office. She couldn't shake how he seemed to know so much about cowboys yet didn't want to talk about them. But seeing him laughing with Jackie and eventually putting her number in his phone calmed Sue's fear that his evening might have been ruined. He was a nice guy and she wanted to see him have a good time. And Jackie genuinely seemed interested in getting to know him.

*****

The annual Friendsgiving celebration was winding down as guests started to gather their coats and casserole dishes while saying their goodbyes and making promises to each other that they would get together more during the year; promises that would mostly go unfulfilled.

Mark found Melanie near the door. "Thanks again for having me. I really enjoyed myself."

"Thank you for coming. I love seeing new faces and I'm glad you had a nice time." She handed him a bag. "Here's some turkey and cranberry salad for a sandwich tomorrow. Put the cranberry salad on the bread with some mayonnaise. Trust me on this. Best turkey sandwich you'll ever have."

Mark smiled as he accepted the bag. "Sounds like it's worth trying. Thank you again." He turned to Sue to thank her as well and gave her a hug. "See you on Monday. Good luck with your research." And then he was out the door, before Sue could ask him if he had remembered any more details about the cowboys he used to know.

Once all the guests were gone, Sue and Jackie helped Melanie with some last-minute clean-up, then put on their coats as Melanie handed them goodie bags. Sue was glad there were enough leftovers that she could have a turkey/cranberry salad sandwich tomorrow. She looked forward to them every year.

"Well, it's time for all our lives to get crazy busy. But we're meeting on Christmas Eve for our annual brunch, right?" Jackie's expression dared either of them to say they couldn't make it. Their Christmas Eve brunch was a tradition that went back farther than the Friendsgiving dinner and it was an extremely rare occasion when one of them was not there.

"I'm already tasting the Christmas pudding!" Melanie exclaimed.

"You know I wouldn't miss it for anything," Sue reassured them. "It's the highlight of my Christmas!"

Jackie looked at Sue with a gleam in her eye. "Unless, of course, you meet a handsome cowboy and we never hear from you again."

Melanie rolled her eyes at her. "One-track mind."

She feigned offence. "A girl can dream, can't she?"

With one last giggle between old friends, they hugged each other and said their goodbyes. Out in the street, Sue pulled her coat tight around her. It was unusually cold for Thanksgiving and there was a bite in the air. She walked to her car and paused as she unlocked the door. A light snow had started to fall. She looked up and felt the flakes as they landed on her face. And for the first time since she was a little girl, found herself opening her mouth to catch snowflakes on her tongue.

*****

Dusty and JoAnne walked into her modest two-bedroom house late on Thanksgiving evening feeling very satisfied after the feast they had enjoyed. Now JoAnne was looking forward to relaxing with Dusty before they both had to go back to work the next day.

"I'm absolutely stuffed!" he exclaimed as he patted his stomach. Even though he probably thought he was sticking it out in exaggeration, trying to look "fat", JoAnne laughed at the notion of Dusty looking like anything other than the trim and fit cowboy he was. At 5' 11" and 170 pounds, there wasn't an ounce of fat on his cut physique. She knew there were plenty of women in town who would gladly give him more than the time of day and JoAnne felt lucky that he wanted to be with her as much as she wanted to be with him. She wasn't tall and skinny and she knew she was no raving beauty but he never looked at her as if she was anything less. When they weren't working crazy hours, they had fun doing just about anything they could think to try. What started out as a mostly fun, "let's hang out together" relationship was quickly turning into love for both of them. After some dubious relationships for JoAnne, she was enjoying one that felt good, satisfying and real.

"Me too. I wanted so much to have another piece of that pecan pie but I just couldn't. I didn't know so much good food could exist on one table."

"You mean one *long* table!" Dusty exclaimed. His boss always held a Thanksgiving feast for everyone on his ranch and several guests since he no longer had any family of his own. And his house was plenty big enough for all the people he invited!

"I don't know how they got it all made and served hot at the same time." she marveled. "I have enough trouble getting four hot plates to one table at the diner!"

Dusty laughed as he walked towards the bedroom with a gleam in his eye. "I don't know about you but I'm ready for bed."

"I'm right behind you." Smiling as she turned off the living room light, she sauntered into the bedroom with expectations of time spent in each other's arms before drifting off to a peaceful sleep when she noticed him take a bottle of pills from his pocket and pop one in his mouth.

"Why are you taking that?" she asked with a disappointed tone. "You certainly don't need it!"

"Don't start. You know it helps me relax." He really didn't want to get into an argument after having such a nice evening that was headed towards an even better ending.

"Yeah, it helps you relax so much you fall asleep."

"Don't exaggerate."

"Why can't I be what relaxes you? Why do you need a pill?" This discussion had definitely not been in her plans for the evening.

"If you'd try it, you'd understand."

"No way. I don't need that crap. And neither do you." She was truly concerned for him since he had been popping pills more often lately. It was his only flaw as far as she was concerned but it was becoming a problem for her. "It's gonna get you in trouble one day."

"You know I'm careful. You worry too much."

"And you don't worry enough." His cavalier attitude was starting to wear on her patience.

"I don't do it enough for anyone on the ranch to notice. But it mellows me out when I need it and it makes me feel good."

"But I don't understand why you feel you need it. You like your job and the people you work with. What do you need to relax from so badly? Don't I make you feel good?"

He looked at her with those blue eyes that always made her melt. "Of course you do. But these help me feel even better."

As he undressed and stretched out in her bed, JoAnne knew it was useless to argue with him. She got undressed and turned out the light. And as she crawled into bed and snuggled next to him, she heard it, softly at first, growing into a steady rhythm...the sound of his snoring. He was already fast asleep.

On nights like this, she wondered why she even asked him to come over.

CHAPTER 4

Sue was on a roll! Following Mark's suggestion to research ranches in Montana and remembering his comments about cowboys, she found The Big M, a large cattle ranch where she made contact with Wayne, the ranch manager. She was pleased when after presenting her idea to him, he was intrigued enough that he agreed to talk with her and also let her spend time on the ranch interviewing any cowpokes who wanted to tell her about their holiday traditions. And he said that if she stayed around long enough she might see some cowboy Christmas traditions first-hand.

She thought the name of the ranch was a little pretentious. *Who names anything "big", unless they are compensating for something?* She contemplated the question as her phone call with Wayne ended. But he seemed nice enough and she was a bit desperate by the time she made contact with him. At that point, she was thrilled to find anyone who would talk about anything cowboys did at Christmas time!

On her way to the airport, Sue stopped by the office to gather some things and hand out a few Christmas gifts. Often when she was on the road doing last minute research, she wouldn't get back to the office until after the holiday and while she only gave gifts to a select few, she hated giving gifts after Christmas unless it absolutely couldn't be avoided. Her editor always received a good bottle of single-malt scotch whiskey, her assistant got exotic scented soaps, lotions and candles that Sue would pick up on her travels throughout the year and the print manager always got something special. While she tried not to, Sue sometimes found herself holding him up in getting the printed articles to press so she tried to make it worth the inconvenience. And for the entire office, she would bake a pan of her mother's recipe for Baklava, a family tradition every Christmas. Sue noted as she walked past the break room that the platter she had placed in there less than 20 minutes prior was already half empty. News of her Baklava traveled fast when it appeared each year!

With her tasks complete, Sue grabbed her laptop and bag, preparing to leave as she felt her phone vibrating in her pocket. Jackie was calling. While she was in danger of getting to the airport late, she never rejected a call from either of her best friends. They always made time for each other. "Hey there. What's up?"

"Guess who's going on their third date this evening?" Jackie sounded like a giddy school girl and before Sue could guess what she had already surmised, Jackie blurted it out. "Me and Mark! Can you believe it?!?"

This explained the smile that Mark was wearing as she glanced at him across the office. Sue was happy her friend was enjoying his company but she hoped it was more than just a fling. "Three dates in less than 2 weeks. That might be a record for you!"

"I'm not *that* bad….am I?"

It was hard for her to tell if Jackie was offended or playing. "Not at all. I'm just happy you two seem to be getting along."

"We really are!" It sounded like Jackie would burst with joy at any moment. "And not just in the usual way I get along with men. He's different."

"How so?"

"There's an air of mystery about him."

"Details please." This was the standard demand within the trio when one of the women was being intentionally coy and holding back vital information.

"He's a great conversationalist. He knows about so much and we talk about all kinds of things. Our goals, our interests, things we want to do, all that. The only odd thing is he doesn't talk about his childhood at all. He asks about mine and seems interested in the most mundane aspects of it but when I ask about his or ask if he had a similar experience to something I've told him, he changes the subject every time."

"Have you asked him why?"

"No, I figure he'll tell me at some point. Maybe he had a tragic upbringing and he doesn't want to reopen old wounds by talking about it. Too early in the relationship to push on something like this. And I want to see where this can go. I really like him!"

"I can tell. And I really am happy for you. Both of you." Sue truly was happy for her friend. But perhaps a little jealous too. She was getting to the age where she'd like to have a man in her life but it just hadn't happened. Her life was good...but not great. Would a man really change that? She'd like to find out but she knew the answer was that only she could make herself truly happy. A man would help but it was up to Sue to change whatever circumstance it was that was holding her back from being content and experiencing the happiness that came with it. But at the moment she was running terribly late! "Mark seems like a nice guy and I hope you have a great time tonight and for many more dates to come. But right now, I need to go."

"I know. Sorry to call during work but I just had to tell you."

"I'm glad you did. Have fun tonight. Talk soon." Sue walked to the exit as she ended the call and glanced at Mark across the open office space. That smile was still there. She had a sense about Jackie's claim that he was holding back about something but concluded that she was probably right. Some memories shouldn't be discussed early in a relationship. And Sue hoped this relationship would last long enough that Mark would feel comfortable talking to Jackie about it. Fingers crossed.

*****

After a mercifully smooth flight during which Sue was able to get some work accomplished, she found herself on Route 87, driving from the Great Falls airport with Spruce, Montana as her destination in a rental car that had a slight hint of cigarette smoke. The pine tree air freshener hanging from the rear view mirror did nothing to hide the smell. Her grandparents had smoked and while the odor in the car brought back fond memories of them, it also reminded her of how much she hated the habit since it had killed both of them. The car was bigger than what she was used to driving but since it was the only one available, she didn't have a choice. So there she was, in a big, somewhat smelly car following instructions given to her by the proprietor of the inn to which she was destined since he warned her that her phone's GPS wouldn't work in the area. 'Cell phone signals are spotty at best out here' was how he described it. This portion of the trip wasn't starting out ideally, that was certain.

The scenery along the highway was, however, breathtaking. Sue had visited every state in the union and had seen plenty of beautiful farmland in her travels. But what surrounded her as she drove was beyond her expectations. Flat land broken up by rolling hills and mountains in the distance as far as the eye could see. She imagined the beauty of the fall colors that would have covered the trees a month or two earlier and the lush greenery that would cover those same mountains in a few months. It had been a while since she was surrounded by this type of scenery and it was calming to her, a feeling she had been lacking lately.

Sue's anticipation of her first meeting grew as she progressed towards her destination. After coming up with an idea that she thought worked, the stumbling blocks she encountered in her research and the difficulty she had in finding enough to write about for the print article had her questioning her subject choice. It didn't help that she recently found herself more irritated than usual with no real understanding of why. She loved the holiday season stretching from Thanksgiving into each New Year but lately she wasn't feeling the usual joy she so treasured during the festive season. And it didn't help that the looming deadline was making her start to think this might be the first year she wouldn't have a solid article for the website. The thought of publishing a piece of work that was not up to her standards was a nagging fear she was having trouble shaking. But as she found her mood turning sour as she drove on, she thought about being around real cowboys, on a working ranch, around animals, away from the holiday craziness of the city, even if only for a few days, and her mood brightened considerably. She was looking forward to writing something different this year and knew that she would do whatever it took to put up a blog post that lived up to the potential of her idea. But first, she needed to get settled so she was glad to see a road sign telling her she was only seven miles from her destination. She wanted to be rested and sharp for whatever the next day held in store. From what Mark had said and the limited exposure she had to cowboys, it seemed as though she might have a tough time getting them to open up to her. She could hear them laughing at her now. *Who wants to read about how cowboys celebrate Christmas?!*

Lost in her thoughts, Sue came crashing back to reality as she suddenly felt the steering wheel shaking violently in her hands as the car pulled severely to the right. She immediately pulled onto the shoulder of the highway and got out of the car. Walking around to the passenger side, she was greeted with the sight of a front tire that was flat as it could be and promptly kicked it! *Great! This is not what I need right now!* She took a few long, deep breaths. Fortunately, before she was even allowed to take her driving test when she turned sixteen, her father had taught her how to properly change a tire. In fact, he showed her several things he felt everyone on the road should know about the car they drove. She could change the oil, replace the battery, inspect the belt and a few other things that had come in handy over the years. Not that she ever did any of those things. But she was glad to know some basics about cars when it came time to take hers in for repairs. She felt certain that knowing something about how they work had saved her from being ripped-off by unscrupulous mechanics more than once. But this time, even though it had been a while, she had to put her skills to the test, knowing she could likely change it faster than if she waited for the rental company's roadside assistance to arrive.

Sue found the jack in the trunk under the spare and surprised herself as she remembered the details her father had shown her so she could safely change the tire. 'Make sure the jack is flat on the ground and straight' her Dad had instructed. 'Jack the car up slightly, loosen the lug nuts, then jack the car up until the tire is off the ground.' The process went smoothly and in what seemed like no time, she had to spare on the car. With the last lug nut nice and tight, Sue slowly lowered the car. And as she did, she watched in disbelief as she saw the spare tire was flat as well.

Unbelievable!

She could feel herself getting red, hot and furious. She did NOT need this! She threw the jack handle to the ground, said a few choice words to herself and opened the car door to retrieve her phone. *Oh, someone is going to be having a worse day than me when I get a hold of them!* She punched in the rental company's phone number and waited. And waited. And waited. Realizing she was not hearing any sound to signify there was a phone ringing at the other end, she looked at her phone to find there was no signal. Sue started to walk around, holding her phone in different positions and heights to try and get a signal.

Unbelievable!

As she continued searching in vain for a signal, a large pickup truck pulled up behind her car. A man got out and waved to Sue as he approached. "Hey there. Looks like you've got a bit of a situation here. You OK?" As he got closer, Sue could see the man was ruggedly handsome, with blue eyes that were clear and friendly. His broad shoulders, jeans, western-style shirt and cowboy hat covering a short crop of salt and pepper hair and three-day beard growth made him look every bit the stereotypical cowboy. But his clothes were surprisingly clean so it certainly didn't appear as if he had just stepped off the ranch. The only thing not looking sharp were his boots. They were worn and old and, she imagined, probably very comfortable, which would be why he wore them everywhere. If Sue didn't know better, this was the cowboy of her youthful dreams, come to sweep her away.

Unfortunately, the cowboy of her dreams had arrived when she was not in the mood! "I'm fine. However, my tire is clearly not." While she didn't want to appear rude, Sue's anger and frustration at her current situation showed in her demeanor and tone. Holding up her phone, she continued. "Just trying to call for service."

The man surveyed the situation, seeing the flat tire on the car and a tire laying nearby with the jack on its side and the handle several feet away. Then he looked at Sue and deduced from her clothing and manicured hands that she was likely not well-versed in manual labor. He teasingly said, "Let me guess. Girl from the big city doesn't know how to change a tire." The smile on his face may have indicated he was trying to make light of the situation but Sue was not having it. Adding an insult to her day did not sit well with her at that moment!

"Oh, I know good and well how to change a tire. Which I have just finished doing, only to find that the spare is also flat!" She glared at him, her eyes daring him to challenge her.

Quickly he realized that this was not a woman who couldn't take care of herself. Holding his hands up in surrender, he tried to get out of the hole he was digging for himself after barely starting their conversation. "Sorry miss, I just assumed. And, I see, wrongly so!"

She was over it immediately and shrugged him off. "Don't worry about it. What I need to do right now is get someone on the phone to *discuss* this matter. That's who really deserves to feel my wrath! I'm supposed to have 24 hour roadside assistance but I can't get anyone on the phone."

"Even if you could get a signal, I'm pretty sure the person who isn't on the other end of that phone is already in hiding."

"Well, they can't hide forever! Certainly not from the strongly worded e-mail I'll be sending them very soon."

"E-mail?"

"It's short for electronic mail." Sue couldn't resist adopting a snarky edge to her voice. "Let me guess, boy from the country doesn't know about e-mail?"

He chuckled. "Oh, I know plenty about e-mail. Texting too. But you seem more like a 'march into the president of the company's office and tell him what you think face-to-face' kinda girl to me."

Sue glared at this stranger for several moments and was about to tear him a new one before she started to see the humor in her current situation. After a moment, she smiled slightly. "Yes, that does seem a bit more like my style, I'll admit." A deep breath helped her to calm down a bit.

"Where are you headed?"

"Spruce".

"Oh, that's just up the road. And since it doesn't appear that the roadside assistance is coming anytime soon, why don't I give you and your flat tires a ride into town and get you fixed up?" Extending his hand, he gave her an embarrassed smile. "Don't know what happened to my manners by the way. My name is Jake. Pleased to meet you."

Sue hesitated then shook his hand, which was slightly rough in contrast to his clean clothes. "Nice to meet you. I'm Sue." She smiled bashfully. "I appreciate your offer very much but I don't want to put you out."

"Don't be ridiculous. Can't possibly leave a pretty little lady on the side of the road! My mama would come down from above and beat me with her rolling pin!" Jake smiled and adopted an exaggerated southern accent. "Mama raised me right!"

She chuckled. "Yes, I can see that."

He motioned to the truck. "Go ahead and climb in. I'll throw your tires in the back and have you at Earl's in no time."

"Earl's?"

"He's a friend of mine who happens to own the best garage in town." Jake proceeded to jack up the car and remove the wheel.

While Sue would never feel comfortable accepting this type of help from someone in the city, she has an innate sense about Jake. He seemed genuine...and safe. She retrieved her purse from the car as he swiftly tossed the tires into the bed of his Ford F250. As she climbed into the truck cab, she was greeted by a beautiful yellow lab sitting in the front seat, patiently waiting for Jake. "Well, hello there. What's your name?"

As Jake climbed behind the wheel, he introduced the two. "Sue, this is Bernie. Bernie, this is Sue."

"Pleased to meet you Bernie." Sue started to scratch Bernie behind his ears. "You're a handsome fellow."

"Don't be offended if he's a bit distant towards you. He doesn't tend to take to strangers immediately." But as Jake spoke, his eyes didn't believe what he was seeing. Bernie was already nuzzled up next to Sue, an action heretofore reserved only for Jake, who looked at Bernie is disbelief. "Hmmm, you seem to have made a great first impression!"

"Bernie knows I love animals. We'll get along just fine."

*****

Five minutes after pulling away from Sue's rental car, she, Jake and Bernie rolled into Earl's service station, a typical small town operation with two service bays and 4 gas pumps. There was a large Santa statue with oil stains strategically placed on his red coat and a wrench in his hand standing between the two bay doors. A banner across the front of the building advertised 'Service with a smile is our specialty'. Sue couldn't remember the last time she had any type of service where the person smiled or even acted as though they cared. She would be surprised if Earl was any different.

Jake pulled up near the service bays and parked his truck. Bernie quickly followed him out the driver's door as Sue climbed down from the passenger side. Fortunately there was a stepping bar attached to the truck. Without it, she didn't want to think of

49

how embarrassing she would look getting in and out of the huge vehicle.

A holiday wreath hung on the door Jake pulled opened as he stepped aside so Sue could walk in ahead of him. But Bernie was faster and beat her through, running up to the counter and jumping up to rest his paws on it, tail wagging the entire time.

Earl looked up as a dog appeared in his face. "Hey Bernie!" He was a medium built man with a pleasant face and overalls that weren't very greasy. But the dirt under his fingernails told Sue they had likely caught him between repair jobs. The garage store seemed organized and clean with the distinct odors of gas, oil and grease hanging in the air. A selection of snacks and sodas that could be found in most gas stations was displayed but there were also several jars of homemade pickles for customers to mix and match: Sweet, Dill, Gherkins, Spicy, Spears, all lined up and looking particularly enticing. Sue realized she was starting to get hungry.

With Bernie patiently waiting, Earl reached under the counter, which made the tail wag even harder. When his hand reappeared with a large dog biscuit, Bernie started to actually jump up and down with anticipation. As he gave the treat to Bernie, Earl looked at Sue and smiled. "And who is the lovely addition to this usual party of two?"

"Hey Earl," Jake quickly responded. "This is Sue."

The smile on Earl's face grew even wider as he winked at Sue. "And where has Jake been hiding you?"

"I found her on the side of Route 87, the proud owner of not one but two flat tires."

"Yikes! That is unfortunate." Earl's reply was genuinely sympathetic. "How'd it happen?"

"One was courtesy of a pothole in the road that I didn't see. The other is a product of an inept rental car company!" Sue tried to hide her frustration but was pretty sure she did a lousy job as the contemptuous tone in her voice made her feelings clear.

"Well, I can see they might not be having a good day once you get in touch with them." Earl could easily ascertain Sue was someone who did not suffer fools gladly. But in this case, he knew she was not in the wrong.

Jake motioned outside. "I have the tires in the truck. Think you can get them patched up quickly?"

"No problem! Pretty slow around here today so I'll have you back on the road in no time."

"Thank you so much Earl." Sue softened a bit as she realized that both Earl and Jake seemed genuinely interested in helping her, something she rarely, if ever, encountered back in the city anymore. "I really do appreciate both of you helping me out."

"Glad to do it." Earl quickly replied with a broad smile. "Come on Jake. I'll help you get those tires." They walked to the truck while Sue checked her phone. She had a signal! It was weak but strong enough so she could check her messages. Bernie stayed with her, happy to sit by her side as she scratched his head after finishing off the treat Earl had given him.

"She's cute!" Earl exclaimed, nudging Jake once they were outside.

Jake smiled as they walked towards his truck. While his friend's statement was quite accurate, he hadn't looked at another woman in the years since his wife had been gone. In his mind, no one could hold a candle to her. "Earl, can I trouble you to take Sue back to her car and put the tires on? I have a meeting with the mayor and now I'm running a little late."

"No problem at all." Earl was certain he knew what the meeting was about. "I know how much the town council appreciates all you do to make the annual Christmas festival happen and I'm definitely not going to be the guy who stands in the way of it this year!"

"Thanks buddy. And whatever this costs, put it on my tab."

Earl looked at Jake with a sly smile. "You just can't help yourself, can you?"

Jake smiled shyly and to avoid further discussion, quickly carried a tire to the open garage bay with Earl close behind. As Earl started to work on the first one, Jake walked back to the office to tell Sue goodbye, coming through the door as she was ending a phone call. "You're in good hands from here on out. Earl's working on your tires now and will get you back to your car as soon as they're ready."

"Thank you again Jake for all your help. I'm really not sure what I would have done if you hadn't come along." She hoped her smile reflected the genuine appreciation she felt.

"Oh, someone else would have stopped and helped you out. We're pretty friendly in these parts."

"Just the same, can I do something to repay you?"

He could see she was not used to the kindness of strangers and also someone who didn't like being indebted to anyone. *A strong, independent woman,* Jake thought. "I'm certain you'll help someone someday in a similar manner. That's plenty repayment for me." He turned towards the door. "C'mon Bernie. We gotta get going." Bernie, still by Sue's side, looked up at her with sad eyes. She bent down and gave him one last scritch behind the ears.

"Nice meeting you Bernie." As she straightened up, she looked at Jake. "You too."

He tipped his hat towards her. "My pleasure as well. Maybe I'll see you around." Jake gave a broad smile that revealed dimples in his cheeks Sue was noticing for the first time. And suddenly his blue eyes seemed to sparkle. As he opened the door, Bernie pulled himself away from Sue and followed. She watched as they walked to the truck, climbed in and headed down the road.

*****

Within an hour, one repaired tire was mounted on the car and the other was secured in the trunk when Sue waved goodbye to Earl as she pulled onto the highway. She couldn't believe that Jake had taken care of the bill. She tried to explain to Earl that her company would cover the cost of the repair but he wouldn't hear of it.

"Jake wouldn't be happy with me if I took a cent from you, no matter who was covering the cost." Earl insisted.

As she headed into town to find the inn, she mused. *So far, it seems cowboys are pretty nice. And handsome. Maybe I'll find one a bit closer to my age and Jackie's prediction will come true.* Then Sue realized the absurdity of her fantasy and came back to reality. *Focus!*

*****

"I can't tell you how much we appreciate your generosity!" Mayor Taylor Williams was shaking Jake's hand vigorously in front of the bank. "Your donation will do more than just keep the town's Christmas festival alive this year."

"You know I'm happy to do it Taylor. With the factory shut and everything else that's going on, people need to have something to look forward to."

"True, but you do a lot already. I'm certain there is a limit to even your generosity. But I'm thankful it didn't stop before we could secure the festival celebration."

"I'm a blessed man and I like to share. I can only buy myself so many trucks and horses." Jake tried to make a joke but he knew that the mayor and many others in town were well aware that, with no wife and kids in his life, Jake was lonely and lacking anyone with which to share his fortune. He had made a good life for himself since appearing in town a dozen or so years before from who-knew-where but there had been a lot of lonely times lately.

"Well, please know you are greatly appreciated. See you at the festival." With a smile, Taylor turned to walk back to his office while Jake walked to his truck where Bernie was patiently waiting for him, sitting in the driver's seat. He wasn't sure why but it seemed that Bernie felt it was his job to keep the seat warm until he returned every time they went somewhere. But this time, he kept the seat warm for naught as Jake decided to stay in town for just a bit longer. Bernie didn't have to be told twice to come out of the truck and happily walked by Jake's side as the pair headed towards the diner.

The bell on the door rang its familiar chime as Jake came through with Bernie close behind. "No buddy, you need to wait outside. I'll only be a few minutes." Bernie gave a sad look as JoAnne approached.

"Don't be silly Jake. Bernie is welcome to come in. He's not going to do anything but sit by your side." JoAnne was someone Jake always enjoyed seeing, her spit-fire personality never ceasing to make him smile. "It's great to see you both again. Didn't expect you'd be in here today."

"I had business in town so I couldn't justify not stopping in. Besides, I'm starving. The mayor can certainly stretch out a meeting."

She laughed, knowing exactly what Jake meant. She'd known the mayor all her life since he was her uncle and it was a running joke in her family that he could tell a one-minute story in an hour flat!

"Have a seat anywhere."

Jake slid into a booth, very glad to sit after the long walk he took with the mayor to view the disrepair of the playground and the space for the planned rehab center. There was much to be done in the town and it made his head swim thinking of all the projects that were desperately needing to be completed. But he was happy to help as much as he could. The town was important to him and he believed people appreciated his efforts. If they didn't, he wasn't going to lose any sleep over it. He didn't do it for adulation. He had had enough of that to last a lifetime!

JoAnne set a cup of steaming coffee on the table as Jake settled in. "I'd say this will warm you up but that's not really an issue today, is it?" The unusually mild weather had been an ongoing topic of discussion around town for several weeks.

"Yeah, I don't know that I've ever seen Dusty and everyone working in t-shirts at this time of year."

"They should enjoy it while they can and keep their coats handy. I've seen the weather change pretty quick some years." JoAnne was certain they were still in for a white Christmas. "The usual?"

He looked over the menu as he spoke. "Since I've got some time now, I'm in the mood for something different today."

JoAnne was shocked. He never ordered anything other than his usual: a grilled chicken breast with mayo and Dijon mustard covered in Monterey Jack cheese and grilled onions between two pieces of toasted 12 grain bread. It was a combination prepared especially for him and one she thought both very specific and odd. Then she tried it and realized her favorite customer was onto something. The flavors blended together so well and made a unique and delicious sandwich. She wondered how he came up with it. Eventually the creation made its way onto the menu and was very popular. "The special is slow-roasted pulled-pork with Tony's secret sauce."

"The smile on your face tells me it's pretty good."

She nodded enthusiastically.

"Sold! With a side of crispy sweet potato fries please." Then it was his turn to smile. "And do you still have the best coconut cream pie I've ever tasted?"

"Only one way to find out." She turned to go and give the cook Jake's order but added, "Thanks again for the invitation the other night. We had a great time."

"Happy you could make it. You know you're welcome anytime." Jake liked JoAnne and he was happy she and Dusty had found each other. He thought they worked well together.

She smiled and walked away as he looked out the window at the people passing by. Mothers with their kids; fathers with their sons; everyone heading who knew where. The town always buzzed with excitement around the holidays and it made him smile. As he watched families going about their day, he thought to himself. *Hold on to each other for as long as you can and don't let misunderstandings come between you.* Before he let thoughts of his own family struggles affect his mood, he turned his attention to the wall-jukebox mounted at the end of his booth. *Let's see if I can find some good tunes to play.*

CHAPTER 5

For the second time in two hours, Sue Stevens was riding into the town of Spruce, Montana. But this time she was doing it as originally planned. As she drove down Main Street, she felt as though she was in another of the quaint towns she had visited a hundred times during the holidays. Festive decorations were in every store front window, lights were strung across the road, wreaths hung from every other light pole, people were bustling along as they accomplished their errands...it all seemed too "perfect". *Did I simply find another town that's like all the others* she asked herself? That's what she was trying to avoid and now feared she was just repeating herself...again. But as she drove down a few side streets, she saw some things she didn't usually see in the places she visited. There were empty store fronts, the school playground had several pieces of equipment that had seen better days, a few homes were boarded up and the hands on the clock in the town square showed a time that hadn't been correct for hours. Definitely not a 'picture-book town'.

Turning back on to Main Street, Sue checked her directions to the inn where there was hopefully a comfy room waiting for her. As she arrived, she noted the charm of the building. The large red brick house appeared to have been lovingly restored by its owner. A flickering electric candle with festive greens at the base glowed in each window. A large wreath with a tartan bow hung from the center roof peak and a smaller matching wreath hung on the front door, which was adorned with a thick white pine rope garland. She retrieved her suitcase from the trunk and made her way up a walkway lined with holiday lights along the railing.

Entering the reception area, Sue was greeted by more tasteful decorations adorning the reception desk, a crackling fireplace and the scent of fresh pine mixing with the smell of burning wood. All of it reminded her of the Christmases of her youth. A four foot tall stuffed bear in a Santa suit stood in the corner. The bear was fun and unusual and held her attention so long that she didn't notice the inn's proprietor entering the foyer.

"Good afternoon. Welcome to Holiday House. I'm Zac."

His warm, genuine greeting caught her off-guard. But because her day so far had gone less than to plan, she braced herself for another potential disappointment. "Hi, I'm Sue Stevens. I have a reservation." Her response to Zac's greeting had a bit more of an edge to it that she really didn't want to exude. She just wanted to relax!

"Yes, Miss Stevens, I've been expecting you." Zac placed a reservation card and pen in front of her. "Just sign in here. Your room is all ready." Sue liked the relative ease of checking into a room in small towns. It was definitely a perk of staying at owner-operated establishments.

With the signature complete, Zac grabbed her suitcase and started up the stairs. "Follow me," he said with a smile. The staircase was truly a work of art that had been carefully restored. The handrail had been hand crafted with care and the floor boards were worn but polished. Fresh greens tied with the same tartan ribbon as on the wreaths she observed outside adorned the railing every three feet. As Zac opened the door to her room, Sue was greeted by a fire burning in the fireplace and a mantle adorned with fresh pine, filling the room with its wonderful aroma. Holiday pillows on the bed and chair and a small Christmas tree in the corner glowing with twinkling white lights added just the right festive atmosphere. The beauty of it all made her catch her breath. "I wasn't expecting a room with a fireplace. This is wonderful!"

Zac smiled. "The house was built in the 1800's so a fireplace was the only way to heat each room. I decided to keep that detail when I refurbished everything, even though I changed them all to gas. The house has a modern heating system too." He shrugged. "Some people like a fire to keep them warm; some don't."

"Well, your efforts at retaining the charm of the original house are apparent and appreciated. You should be very proud of your accomplishment."

"Thank you very much. That means a lot coming from you." He smiled bashfully.

She hesitated. "I'm thinking you might know a bit more about me than I was intending to reveal." Sue usually didn't use her real name when making reservations in towns where she was doing research, so that no one would treat her differently than a regular guest. But when she made this reservation, she knew she wasn't going to be writing about the inn or even the town so she didn't figure it was necessary to hide her identity. Now she was rethinking that decision.

"Sorry, don't mean to make you uncomfortable. But my sister is a huge fan of yours and when she saw your name in the reservation book, she freaked out."

Sue gave a slight laugh. "Oh, I'm sure you're exaggerating."

"Not in the least! You'll see. She works at the best diner in town so you won't be able to avoid her if you want good food while you're here." Zac smiled as he warned. "Once you walk in there, you won't get her to stop talking to you."

Damn! Definitely not what Sue was hoping for on this trip. She really didn't want to deal with fans this year. While most travel writers don't have the issue, Sue was "fortunate" enough to have people get truly excited about her visits in a lot of the places she explored. But it often made her work harder. *Why can't this year be different?* Still, Zac seemed like a decent, genuine person so she held out hope that his sister would be the same. "Well, I hope I don't disappoint her. I'm not here to write about the town, which I think might be a good thing. With an inn named 'Holiday House', I'm starting to think I'm in a town that's like a lot of other quaint towns I've visited where everything is picture-perfect and they make a big to-do of every holiday, especially Christmas."

Zac lowered his head. "Well, now I hope *we* don't disappoint. We're a town of hard-working people. We really don't have time to 'make a big to-do' about anything."

Sue realized she was not getting off on the right foot. *What's wrong with me??* "Sorry, I didn't mean to insult. I really need for my article to be special this year so I guess I'm putting a lot of pressure on myself. I just have to get it right."

"No need to apologize. I imagine even world-renowned writers like yourself have difficult days like the rest of us." Zac smiled and winked.

Sue laughed out loud. "Well-known I'll give you. 'World-renowned' is a stretch!"

"Well, from what my sister tells me, you're a big deal in the travel writing industry so I'll follow her advice and make sure you have whatever you need during your stay, just in case you decide to mention Holiday House in your article."

"OK, I have to ask about the inn's name. It just reeks of small-town quaintness. How did you come up with it?"

Zac blushed and smiled. "My wife came up with it. I told her it was corny but she's Scottish and they don't call vacations a 'vacation'. They call them 'holidays'. So, this is basically Vacation House!"

She smiled genuinely. "Now that makes sense!" Sue dug into her purse for a pen before realizing there was one along with note paper on the antique desk in the room. She sat down and looked at Zac. "Before you go, I'm hoping you can give me some directions. My cell phone doesn't seem to be working too well."

Zac let out a knowing chuckle. "That's because this is 'The Big M'. People come out here to get away from everything, especially cell phones, which is good because cell service out here is not the best!"

"Is everything here called 'The Big M'?

He gave her a puzzled look.

"I'm looking for a ranch called 'The Big M'."

"Oh, that's easy to find. It's just outside of town. Take Main Street and get on 87 going west. Take you about 20-25 minutes to get to the main house."

She looked at him quizzically. "I thought you said it was just outside of town."

"It is. But it's a big ranch!" Zac picked up a remote control from the fireplace mantle and held it up. "Use this to turn the fire on and off and breakfast starts at 7:00 am. If you need anything, just pick up the phone to let me know." He quickly left the room, closing the door behind him.

Sue wasn't sure what to make of Spruce, Montana. Everyone she met so far had been very nice, seemingly regular small town people. In many ways, the town looked like so many others she had visited over the years. But she had a sense that things here were different. Hopefully she would be able to get what she needed.

*****

Sue unpacked and got settled in the room. She appreciated the coziness of the inn so much she decided to figure out a way to include it in her article. She plugged in her laptop so it would be charged and ready to go after she returned from interviewing the cowboys she was set to meet the next day. Suddenly, she realized she was hungry. Actually, she was famished! Because of her tire issues, she hadn't eaten since breakfast and now that it was after 6 pm, she needed to find a decent meal. She walked down to the reception area to find Zac doing paperwork. He told her how to find 'the best diner in town' and she decided to walk since he assured her she would want to walk back in order to work off the meal.

Exiting the inn, Sue noted the weather seemed unseasonably mild for Montana in December. Though not an expert, she was certain this weather was not typical for the time of year. Mark had all but assured her Montana always had a white Christmas. But it seemed as though it was a real possibility for that to not be the case this year.

As she walked down the street, Sue was greeted by passersby with smiles and 'hellos' that she missed when she was in the city. She wondered why city dwellers couldn't take the time to simply acknowledge each other as they passed. It took little time or effort and people in small towns always seemed to genuinely enjoy greeting total strangers. *Why can't everyone do it* she thought? She felt certain that a pleasant greeting could easily brighten someone's day. So she did her part as she walked through the streets of Spruce.

Following Zac's instructions, Sue found The Starlight. As she entered, she found a diner that wasn't typical of the many small towns she had visited over the years. The first thing she noticed was this diner did not have cheesy Christmas decorations hanging everywhere. It was rare that she saw a diner without a cheap artificial tree at the door that looked like it had seen better days and dime store paper Santa, reindeer and wreath cut outs plastered everywhere. And elves perched on every shelf ledge! The Starlight was different...and classy! A natural Christmas tree stood cheerily by the entrance and a natural pine garland was draped along the entire length of the wall facing the seating counter. An electric candle was in each window and realistic artificial greens were in the center of every table. Christmas music played in the background and the sound of conversation mixed with enticing odors coming from the kitchen. In fact, the food smelled so good, even if she had to put up with Zac's fan of a sister, Sue determined this was the place to be. As she waited to be seated, the eyes of the woman walking up to greet her grew wide with excitement.

"Sue Stevens! Hi! I can't believe you're actually here!" She was obviously excited but tried to keep her voice down as she greeted Sue like an excited kid meeting the mall Santa at Christmas. "I'm JoAnne. My brother told me you were coming to town but I just can't believe you're here. I'm a huge fan! I'm so excited to meet you!" The words were tumbling from her mouth so fast that Sue hardly had time to comprehend everything JoAnne said as she shook her hand vigorously.

"Hi JoAnne. Zac told me you were a fan but I thought he was exaggerating about how much of one." JoAnne still hadn't let go of her hand. "It's a pleasure to meet you." She was trying not to let this greeting turn into a scene. Fortunately, everyone nearby took little notice of JoAnne's excitement as Sue managed to get her hand back.

"I'm sorry, I don't mean to gush. But I really do enjoy your work. You've stirred up a desire in me to travel and see as much of this world as I can."

Sue appreciated JoAnne's enthusiasm. "Then I have accomplished my goal," she said with a warm smile.

"Come this way. I have a relatively quiet table for you." JoAnne led the way to a table in a section of the diner that wasn't overly crowded, although Sue noted that the diner was busy for the mid-week. A sign the food was good! She appreciated the quiet and solitude of the table and couldn't wait to peruse the menu JoAnne handed her after she sat.

"The special tonight is meatloaf. I know, it doesn't sound very special but you're in the heart of beef-country and trust me, it's spectacular. What can I get you to drink? We have the best-stocked bar in town and an outstanding bartender!" Sue found JoAnne's enthusiasm infectious.

"After the day I've had, I think I deserve a nice single-malt scotch but you most likely don't have Balvenie, do you?" She had developed a palette for fine Scotch whiskey during her European travels and indulged when she could.

"Well, this will impress Jackson. He rarely has anyone ask for this by name." JoAnne's smile broadened even more. "You want that neat or on the rocks?"

"One rock please. Just enough to open up the flavor."

"Oh, you just scored major points again with Jackson. He's going to want to meet you!" JoAnne walked to the bar as fast as she could without running. Her excitement at Sue's presence had yet to wane!

As Sue waited for her drink, she noticed that "Looking For Christmas" by Clint Black was playing in the background. A favorite album of hers, this particular song struck her at that moment. Sue *was* searching for Christmas. A *different* Christmas. She listened to the lyrics as she contemplated her life. What else was she searching for?

Her train of thought was broken by JoAnne returning, still on cloud nine, with her drink. "As I predicted, Jackson was impressed with your selection. He'll probably stop by to make sure you're enjoying it! Have you decided on what you'd like?"

Sue looked up from the menu. "I learned long ago that when someone enthusiastically recommends a certain food item to go with that recommendation and I've rarely been disappointed. So, meatloaf it is."

"You won't be disappointed this time either! And if it's not asking too much, I'd love to talk to you about your travels, if you have some time while you're in town."

Sue was flattered by JoAnne's interest in her work and sensed that she was a wandering soul in search of places to see. "Of course. You know where I'm staying. And since your brother tells me this is the best diner in town, I'm sure we'll be seeing a lot of each other. We'll find time to chat."

JoAnne was elated! "One meatloaf dinner coming up." She turned towards the kitchen and was gone in a flash.

*****

That may well have been the best meatloaf I've ever had Sue told herself as she left the Starlight. Never something that Sue ever thought of as special, the cook managed to make the mundane truly delicious and satisfying. It helped that the side dish of mashed sweet potatoes with cinnamon and brown sugar was delicious as well and the sautéed mushrooms were prepared to perfection. She had wanted dessert, expecting it to be equally satisfying, but simply didn't have room for anything else. She was thankful now she had taken Zac's advice to walk. She definitely needed to get some exercise after that meal!

The evening temperature was still unseasonably mild as she made her way back to the inn. She again noticed several empty store fronts as she walked. It struck her as sad that many of the small towns that were so important to the building of the country in the 1900's were vanishing from the landscape as their businesses failed or moved. Modernization and foreign sourcing of goods had shuttered so many businesses and, therefore towns. As a rule, people don't live where there is no work unless they already have money and Sue had learned through her travels that many people who lived in small towns were loath to relocate and she couldn't find fault in their thinking. Some rural areas simply had charms that most big cities did not. She knew there were benefits to both city and small town living but lately she found herself viewing small towns as having an advantage.

Before she knew it, she was back at the inn and...exhausted. No longer feeling stuffed from dinner, she made her way to her room, switched on the fire and got ready for bed. A warm bath helped her relax and the coziness of the room gave her a warm feeling inside. The day had been tiring and could have ruined her mood, which was easy to do these days. But the kindness of a stranger or two turned everything around. Sue crawled under the thick down comforter and felt a reassuring warmth she hadn't felt for quite some time. Something about this small town was different to her. But before she could pin-point that difference, she drifted off to a deep sleep.

*****

Jake sat in his favorite chair, the one in which he used to snuggle with his wife, and stared at the empty fireplace. It always relaxed him to stare at a dancing fire and even though it was too warm to have a roaring fire at the moment, he stared at the fireplace anyway. Bernie was comfortably curled up in his bed, catching up on the rest he missed during their busy day.

What a day it had been! Stopping to help someone possibly in distress on the side of the highway was nothing new for him. He always stopped when faced with that type of scene and was never surprised when city dwellers that were passing through were hesitant to accept help or sometimes wouldn't even admit they needed it. He wondered why some people had a hard time accepting help from others. But when he stopped to help today he hadn't expected Sue. Beautiful, strong, independent and seemingly intelligent. All the attributes he liked in a woman. The same qualities his wife had. Except Sue seemed to be a bit negative. Perhaps that was to be expected considering the circumstances under which they met. And she had loosened up a bit during their brief ride to Earl's so he hoped her mood was just a result of the day's events. She was too attractive to be so negative.

Meeting her had stirred something inside Jake. While he hadn't given much thought to the fact that he was alone during the last several years, he was, in fact, lonely. Meeting Sue seemed to bring to the forefront of his thoughts what he had been pushing to the back of his mind for quite some time. Maybe it was time to get out and socialize again. The business was in good hands and he didn't need to be around all the time. He could afford to take at least a little time for himself. Dolly, his faithful housekeeper, cook and friend, had suggested it many times but he always dismissed her. Now he was starting to think she had a point. Too bad the woman who got his thoughts on track was a bit young for him. Or was she? Sue appeared to be no more than 35 but it was hard to tell these days. He had always had a hard time telling people's ages, probably because in another life he had always been surrounded by people who made it a point to look anything but their real age. Some wanted to look older, most wanted to look younger. But it didn't really matter. Sue was passing through and he needed to find someone closer to his own age, although he was doubtful he would ever find someone with his similar experiences. But that wasn't a bad thing.

CHAPTER 6

Sue awoke earlier than needed but got out of bed anyway since she didn't want to waste any time. After an unusually peaceful night's sleep, she enjoyed a delicious breakfast in front of the inn's grand dining room fireplace. The omelet of farm-fresh eggs with spinach and cheese that was light, fluffy and delicious! Along with fresh-sliced bread toasted to a golden brown and coffee with a hint of nutmeg, the meal started Sue's day off right. After checking her directions one last time with Zac, she set out for The Big M.

Seemingly the only person on the road, Sue found herself growing nervous with anticipation as she approached her destination. Not because she was about to interview people she didn't know. That was nothing new. But she hadn't been around horses and animals in general for a long time. She missed having four-legged friends in her life and hoped she'd be able to resist spending more time with them than the humans she was going there to see!

After a solid 30 minutes of driving, she finally saw what she hoped was the entrance to the ranch. She had been driving past fenced pastures for miles and wondered if they belonged to The Big M. She had seen a herd of cattle several miles back so if they were part of the ranch, it was, indeed, a large spread.

Sue turned into the entrance and passed under an archway that confirmed she was in the right place. The large letters spelling out the ranch's name seemed appropriate. It *was* big! She drove up a seemingly endless driveway until finally arriving at a cluster of buildings. The largest building was obviously the main barn but there were also two bunkhouses, a large stable and several storage sheds, all painted the traditional barn-red color she had seen many times in western movies. A large riding arena told Sue they trained horses in addition to raising cattle on this impressive spread. Silos rose above the cluster of buildings and there was a large house on top of a small hill set apart from everything else. Sue assumed it to be the home of the ranch owner and wondered if he or she was a pretentious, faux cowboy or the real deal. Seeing the attention to detail of the house and the yard around it, she decided on faux. She parked her car and climbed out to the stares of several of the men and woman working steadily around the barn. One of them stopped his work to watch her. Extending her hand, Sue smiled as she approached him. "Hi, I'm Sue Stevens, looking for Wayne." The cowboy stood silent for a few moments, not seeming to comprehend what she had said.

"Sorry ma'am." Tipping his hat and removing his leather gloves to shake hands, he seemed too shy to talk to a woman. "I'm Cowboy Bill. Didn't mean to stare. We just don't get a whole lotta ladies out here."

She was glad her first encounter with a cowboy was not at all what she had anticipated and smiled. "Glad I could break up the monotony. Is Wayne around?"

"No ma'am. He ain't here."

This wasn't the news she wanted to hear, having made an appointment just so this wouldn't happen. "I don't understand. I'm supposed to speak with him this morning."

"Yes ma'am. He had an emergency. Told me you'd be comin' and said to give you his apologies and tell you he'll be available tomorrow if you can come back."

"Well, I guess I don't have a choice." Frustration was obvious in her tone. *So much for the day going smoothly.* To Sue, this was par for the course on how this project had been going so far!

Cowboy Bill motioned towards the house. "Wayne said you should feel free to go on up to the big house and talk to the owner. Maybe he can help you. Sorry, I shoulda told you that sooner."

Sue looked at the house. *How is a pretentious, pretend cowboy going to help me?* But if she wanted to talk to some of the cowboys to try and salvage the day, she figured she didn't have a choice but to talk to the owner. *Better to get permission than get thrown off the ranch!*

"Thank you Bill. I'll do just that."

"Welcome ma'am. And, please, call me 'Cowboy Bill'. I wouldn't know to respond if someone just called me 'Bill'." He shrugged slightly. "Been 'Cowboy Bill' forever."

Sue could see he was shy, nervous and sorry he corrected her all at once. She found Cowboy Bill charming and he soothed the growing frustration she felt. "Sorry. Cowboy Bill it is. And please, call me Sue. I like to think I'm too young to be called 'Ma'am', although maybe that's not the case anymore." A broad smile flashed across his face as she turned towards the house.

As she walked up the hill, she realized just how large it was. The front porch was deceiving from a distance since it was very deep and appeared to stretch around 3 sides of the house. Behind it was a large, multi-level home which seemed as though it could house everyone working on the ranch and then some! Large rough-hewn logs made up the exterior of the structure giving it an authentic ranch-house appearance that made her wonder if they completed the look inside or if the interior had a modern-wall finish. She could picture the rooms as being huge, grand expanses and it was very likely her entire apartment could fit into the study of this Montana ranch house! Sue felt it was more and more likely the ranch was owned by someone who hadn't gotten his hands dirty...ever. The gardens around the house were obviously well tended and the furniture on the porch was sturdy and appeared expensive. *This guy probably indulges his every whim he can conjure up while everyone around him does all the actual work* she thought as she walked to the door. She realized she was being negative but with her plans for the day foiled, she wasn't feeling particularly charitable towards others.

A large, simple green wreath with no ribbon or bow for adornment hung at the center of the massive entry door. *Simple elegance...on a ranch?!?* Not what she expected.

Sue knocked and waited as she heard a dog bark, getting louder as it approached the door. Seconds later the door opened and a yellow lab came bounding out. She looked down in surprise. "Bernie?" She bent down to pet him, then she looked up to see Jake standing in the doorway as her mouth dropped open in disbelief.

"Hey there. We meet again," he said, grinning broadly.

Sue collected herself enough to stop staring and close her mouth. "Hey there yourself. What are you doing here?" She realized how silly her question sounded as it was coming out of her mouth.

"I live here," Jake laughed. "What are you doing here?"

She was feeling a bit flustered at the unexpected surprise. "Sorry, I was supposed to meet Wayne to interview him for an article I'm writing."

"That's you?" Now it was Jake's turn to be surprised. "Wayne mentioned a reporter would be coming by but I had no clue it would be you. Guess it makes sense though since you were obviously not looking to relocate out here when I met you yesterday."

"Well, it's true when they say 'it's a small world'. I would never have guessed you were the owner of the The Big M."

"Not sure how to take that."

"Sorry, I didn't mean that the way it probably sounded. I just thought you were a nice person who stopped to help someone in distress. Not the owner of a ranch like this."

"Believe it or not, people with money can actually be nice too." Jake was enjoying toying with her but did it with a smile.

Sue was digging herself a hole she would not soon be able to climb out of if she kept it up! "I'm really making a mess of this!" she stammered. "I don't know what I was expecting when I knocked on this door. To be honest, I don't know that I ever planned to meet the owner of the ranch. I just wanted to talk to some cowboys for my article and go home." She tried to hide her frustration but failed more than she realized. "This whole trip has not gone according to plan so far!"

"I'm starting to think that the big, bad city has made you jaded." With a knowing tone, he added, "It can happen."

He was right. Sue had developed a pessimistic edge to her attitude lately that was out of character and certainly didn't belong in a place where she had met nothing but genuinely nice people. "Well, I apologize sincerely if I insulted you or insinuated anything negative. And I'm actually thankful that it's you who lives here so I can thank you in person for your help and generosity yesterday. Earl wouldn't allow me to pay. He told me you took care of everything. That was unnecessary but very much appreciated. Thank you."

"You're very welcome. Glad I came along when I did." Jake stood aside. "Please come in and get warmed up, even though it's not very cold today."

Sue entered the house and stood in what could only be described as a *grand* foyer, realizing she had been right. Her entire apartment could fit in this one space! The ceiling was vaulted up two stories and a wrought iron light fixture hung in the center. The floors and walls were natural wood and a large solid wood beam ran the entire length of the ceiling into the main part of the house. Jake took her coat and hung it on a sturdy peg, one of many lining the wall behind the door. She followed Jake and Bernie into a great room which matched the grandness of the foyer. A huge space with more vaulted ceilings and large windows overlooking the ranch, the room was filled with classic leather farmhouse-style furniture that looked as comfortable is it did sturdy. Area rugs sparsely covered the natural wood floors. Tasteful Christmas decorations were scattered throughout the room, of which the fireplace was the obvious centerpiece. Natural stone expertly put together made up the grand fireplace that covered the entire wall at the end of the room. The area for the fire itself seemed larger than most and an impressive stack of dried wood was piled next to it, ready to be burned. It was clear to see it was a labor of love and built to impress. Sue imagined the stones making up the structure were likely harvested from the very land where the house stood. A thick wood beam matching the beams in the ceiling made up the mantle, which was adorned with a thick garland of fresh white pine, sugar pine cones and twinkling lights woven throughout. The only thing missing was a Christmas tree.

Jake motioned to the couch facing the fireplace. "Please, have a seat and make yourself comfortable."

As Sue sunk into the deep, soft tan leather couch, Bernie snuggled up to her on the floor, using one of her feet as a pillow. She couldn't help but imagine the festive gatherings that could be held in a room this size. "I have to say, this is an impressive room. Actually, can I call it a *room*?"

Jake flashed an embarrassed smile. "It is a bit large. But it gets filled up now and then. Can I get you something to drink?

"No thanks, I'm fine."

Jake settled into his leather chair near the fireplace. "So Wayne told me you're doing research for an article."

"Yes, I write for a travel magazine and I'm looking for an authentic cowboy or two. But I never expected to find someone like you when I was told I could find one here."

"Someone like me?!? C'mon now." Jake feigned great offense while smiling. "Cowboys aren't like you probably imagine. We speak in full sentences, help ladies in distress and we even know how to send e-mails!"

Sue laughed. "Duly noted."

"OK, serious question. Why does a travel writer need to interview a real cowboy? The two topics don't seem to match up."

"Yes, I can see where there might be confusion. If you have a few minutes I'll explain."

Jake settled back in his chair. "Fire away."

As Sue explained the idea behind her article, it was obvious that he had never heard of her and that the business of travel writing was something he likely never considered. But Jake listened intently, asking an occasional question that proved he was actually interested. After she had shared her reason for being there, Sue decided that maybe this unlikely cowboy could provide context for her article. "Would you mind answering a few questions?"

"Why not?!"

Thankful her trip to the ranch wasn't looking like a waste after all, Sue quickly dug into her purse and retrieved her recorder, note pad and pen. "Let's start with the ranch. Has it been in your family long?"

"No Ma'am. My wife and I bought it about a dozen years ago."

"So it's safe for me to assume you haven't been a rancher all your life then. What made you decide to change course?"

"It was my wife's idea. She thought it was time to get out of the city, move somewhere that we could raise our kids in a place where the pace was slower and family values were strong. Where there is a real sense of community and folks actually respect each other. The city will eat you alive if you let it and we wanted something better for our kids. So, we bought the beginnings of this ranch."

"The beginnings?"

"We got a couple hundred acres to get started and were pretty lucky in our first couple of years. Before long, we had a solid herd of cattle and things rolled along pretty quickly."

"Sounds like you put together a nice family business."

"Don't be fooled by what you see in the movies. Ranching looks like fun but it's a lot of back-breaking work! Not a life for the faint-of-heart."

That's the second time someone has told me that in the last couple weeks Sue thought. "What makes it so difficult?"

"The physical labor for starters. Then you have the federal and state regulations to keep track of and follow, animal rights activists, disease, drought, rising fuel and feed costs and a hundred other things that can discourage you every day if you let them. It's really a life only for people who love nature, enjoy overcoming challenges and have a knack for solving problems. Most people would go running for the hills."

"So if it's that difficult, why do you do it?"

A broad smile came across Jake's face. "Because I love nature, enjoy overcoming challenges and have a knack for solving problems. And I can't run up a hill to save my life!"

For the brief period she had known Jake, Sue knew that last statement couldn't possibly be true. His trim figure told her that he was more active than men half his age. "Well, ranching seems to suit you. From what I understand, The Big M is one of the largest ranches in the state so you must be very adept at overcoming the challenges thrown your way. And I'm assuming it's a family operation so it's good you have help in running such a large operation."

"Everyone that works on the ranch is family to me. Doesn't matter if we're blood or not. And we all work hard, harder than I ever did living in the city. We raise cattle, cut horses, grow crops and a whole lot more."

"So what is involved in that 'whole lot more'?"

"Hold on to your saddle." Jake knew the tidbit of information he was about to throw her way would to lead to a lot more questions. "We host cowboy-themed vacations!"

It was hard for Sue to hide her stunned surprise."OK, I know I'm just learning about all this but isn't that a little unusual?"

"Again, my wife was the culprit. She loved it here so much and she figured we had the space to host folks who would like to come here and experience what we do every day."

"The simple life of a farming family."

Jake let out a booming laugh. "Make no mistake, there is nothing simple about it but we let the guests get involved as much as they want, helping out with chores and projects that are always needing to be done. Mostly my wife wanted for folks to be able to know the peace we enjoy out here, away from the craziness of work and their own daily responsibilities. Even when we're workin' and sweatin', moving the cattle, branding them, keeping them safe from wolves and whatever, there's a peace living out here brings me that I've never known before. I wouldn't give up this life for anything and we wanted people to be able to experience it, even if only for a brief period."

Sue busily made notes on her pad. After writing for several moments, she was eager to find out more. She wasn't expecting something like this! "So what should people expect to experience during a 'Cowboy-themed vacation'?"

"Something they aren't likely to forget," Jake stated confidently. "There is always plenty of work to be done and the guests can join in if they want. Some people have a natural knack for ranch work and others might need to be coaxed out of their comfort zone. But they all enjoy it once they get comfortable and everyone leaves here with a better appreciation of what we do. And when folks come during a holiday, well, that's a real fun time for everyone involved. The work we do makes everyone appreciate the holidays that much more because hard work makes for harder play! We have special things that we do for every holiday, especially Christmas. That was my wife's favorite so she always made sure to do something special for our guests."

Sue hesitantly inquired. "You said Christmas *was* her favorite holiday?"

Jake's demeanor changed slightly. "She's been gone five years. Cancer."

"I'm so sorry!"

He looked away for a moment. "It is what it is and there was nothing I could do to change anything." He started to give more details but thought better of the idea, not wanting to spoil a conversation he was enjoying so much.

As a journalist, Sue had learned long ago that sometimes awkward subjects came up during an interview and unless it was the main topic, it was best to move on from it as quickly as possible to avoid embarrassing the interviewee. "So you kept up the holiday celebration traditions?" Fortunately, it seemed to work with Jake.

As Jake reflected, a smile returned to his face. "Yeah, Mary wanted me to keep things going. She loved it here so much and felt it was a way she could live on at the ranch so we still do many of the traditions she started. In fact, we still host a Christmas Eve party every year that winds up with a walk under the moonlight just before midnight to welcome Christmas under the stars overlooking a snow-covered field. She loved doing that every year and so do our guests, even the ones from Spruce. But to be honest, I think people like the spiked hot apple cider just as much as the midnight walk! Maybe more."

"Sounds like a truly wonderful tradition." Sue mused. "Perhaps the first cowboy Christmas tradition for my article,"

"Being out in the fresh air, under the stars is a simple, basic 'cowboy' thing but, like I said, there's a peace out here that's hard to find anywhere else."

Sue's notepad was quickly filling up but she continued questioning Jake. "So I'm assuming you had a Thanksgiving vacation gathering this year. What did your guests experience?"

"I'll answer your question after you answer one for me. What did you do for Thanksgiving?"

Not sure where he was going with his inquiry, Sue happily recounted the festivities at Melanie's Friendsgiving celebration, providing details about the evening that she felt would reflect the uniqueness of the yearly celebration, even mentioning the new employee who told her Montana was the place to find cowboys *and* have a white Christmas. Sue still wasn't sure how a 'city boy' knew so much about ranches and cowboys. After recounting the details of her holiday, she posed to Jake, "So what did your guests experience?"

"Pretty much the same thing!" Jake replied with a sly smile.

The look that Sue gave him clearly expressed her disbelief.

"I'm not kidding! For years we had guests come for the Thanksgiving holiday who didn't know each other and every year, they left as friends who kept in touch throughout the year and meet up back here for Thanksgiving whenever they can. The group has grown so much that I had to stop taking reservations from anyone who hadn't been here in previous years. We always have a huge, traditional Thanksgiving dinner with turkeys raised on the ranch and people bring their favorite dishes or cook them here. We watch football, play football, tell stories by the fire and catch up with each other. It's the ultimate Friendsgiving celebration!"

"It does sound wonderful." Sue marveled as she continued to make notes. Another day that seemed like a failure had again been rescued by Jake, who provided significant substance for the article, even if it might take her project in a slightly different direction. She felt a sense of relief as she looked at her watch. "Jake, I truly thank you for your time but I think I've taken up enough of it. I'm sure you have things you need to get done and I need to get my notes in order. You really have provided me with a lot of great information. Thank you very much!"

"My pleasure Sue." Jake smiled at her as he realized he hadn't talked to a woman this much since Mary had passed. "I enjoyed this diversion."

"Is it OK for me to stop by tomorrow and speak with Wayne and your cowboys to get some details on their Christmas traditions?"

"Sure, no problem. But don't forget about the cowgirls. We got them too!"

"Noted." Sue was impressed that there was more to this ranch, and likely its owner, than what she first imagined. She gathered her things and stood up. Bernie was not happy at losing his resting place but followed Sue and Jake to the door, tail wagging all the time. As Jake helped Sue with her coat, she suddenly felt awkward. And she wasn't sure why.

"Be careful getting back to town. No flat tires today!"

"That's the plan. Thanks again for your time. Hope I see you tomorrow." She felt awkward again. Why had she said that? She wasn't returning to talk with Jake. She blushed and looked down as she left the house and hurried to her car without looking back.

Jake watched as she walked down the stairs, across the grass, got into her car and drove off. As he watched her car disappear down the driveway, he realized she was the first woman he had spent any real time talking with since his beloved Mary passed. He had forgotten how enjoyable something as simple as conversation with the opposite sex could be. It wasn't that he had avoided such activity. He just hadn't sought it out. *Maybe it's time for that to change.*

*****

Jake was about to turn and go back into the house when he heard some sort of excitement in the corral. Knowing Wayne had been pulled away to take care of personal business, he wanted to be certain the boss's absence wasn't being taken advantage of. As he turned the corner of the barn, he could see Dusty, one of the cowboys who showed real promise, whooping it up, riding his horse around the corral as fast as he could with no apparent purpose other than to show off. A few of the other cowpokes were laughing and egging him on at one end of the corral but as soon as they saw the big boss come out from behind the barn, they quickly lost interest and dispersed.

Jake didn't like seeing the animals worked for nothing. *Animals are to be respected* he thought. *We need them as much as they need us.* He approached the edge of the corral and leaned on the fence. When Dusty flew by the first time, he could see Jake wasn't smiling. On his second pass, Jake waved him over. By the time Dusty got the animal to a full stop, he was down at the other end of the corral. Jake waited patiently.

"What's up boss?" Both the horse and Dusty were panting heavily.

"Not so sure running this animal so fast for no reason is the best use of your time. Or the horse's energy." Jake's stern demeanor should have indicated to Dusty he was to knock it off immediately. But the cowboy seemed oblivious to his boss's displeasure.

"Just havin' a little fun."

Jake had seen this kind of thing before, in another life, and had hoped when he moved to the ranch he wouldn't have to deal with it ever again. "Not sure you're paid to have fun."

"Gotta have some fun boss. Makes getting up in the morning worthwhile."

For someone who had made a strong first impression when he arrived, Dusty was going downhill. Fast. "I think you have plenty of reasons to get up every day. You're dating a fine woman, you earn an honest wage, people depend on you."

"All true."

"So save the fun for your time off, not for when you're getting paid. You out of things to do for the day?"

"Oh, I'm sure there's somethin' that needs doin'."

Jake was not amused by the continuing aloofness he was seeing. "Then get back to work. And never work my animals for your amusement or anyone else's." With a glare that dared Dusty to make one more smart-ass comment, Jake stared him down. Dusty's goofy expression didn't change as he started towards the barn where his duties awaited, seemingly without a care in the world. That would change soon. This needed to be dealt with immediately upon Wayne's return. They both felt Dusty had potential but that didn't matter. Jake would not tolerate this kind of behavior, no matter who was involved. *I came here to get away from this crap.*

CHAPTER 7

Sue was glad to be on her way back to The Big M. Even though she didn't talk to Wayne as planned, she was content the previous day hadn't been a total loss. Her conversation with Jake provided an unexpected option. Worried that her readers might not accept the print and website articles both being about non-traditional jobs at Christmas, the fact that Jake hosted cowboy-themed vacations at his ranch would allow her to make part of her article more like the traditional Christmas fare her followers were used to, if she felt it was needed. But now she was headed towards the ranch to do her main interview with Wayne and, hopefully, some of the cowboys and cowgirls working on the ranch. She was very curious to learn if the traditions were the same between the sexes.

She had called Wayne before she left the inn, just to be sure she wouldn't be wasting another trip. He promised he'd be waiting for her and as she drove up to the main barn, she saw a weathered but fit cowboy she hadn't noticed the day before, figuring it had to be Wayne. He looked every bit the typical cowboy as he leaned on a post, seemingly directing the organized chaos around him as everyone went about their various tasks. He was dressed in traditional cowboy garb: Dungarees, a western-style shirt, cowboy hat and, like Jake, well-worn boots that probably should have been replaced long ago but were just as likely too comfortable to give up. His pure white hair was longer than she expected, reaching below his collar line and he had a rather large sheath attached to his belt with a bone-handled knife safely tucked inside. She imagined he was probably anxiously awaiting her arrival so he could be done with her silliness and get back to work. Undeterred and not knowing exactly what to expect, she got out of the car, walked straight up to him with a smile on her face and her hand extended. "You must be Wayne."

A warm smile came across his weathered face as he shook Sue's hand. "And you must be the writer I've been hearing so much about!"

"How'd you guess?"

"Main giveaway if the fact that we don't get a lot of pretty ladies visitin' out here."

As the words left his mouth, one of the cowgirls walked by. "And what am I, the ugly duckling?" Even though she was smiling, Sue wasn't sure if she was offended or playing.

Wayne pleasantly dismissed her comment. "Oh go on Stacey. I see you every day. And you're still the best lookin' cowpoke out here!" Sue was certain his statement was accurate. Stacey may have been wearing a dusty flannel shirt and dungarees with muddy leather chaps but her soft features shown through and it was easy to see that she would clean up nicely. Her dirty blonde hair was woven into a long braid that ran down her back almost to her waist and her blue eyes could easily entice any cowboy she set them upon!

"Damn right!" Stacey laughed as she walked over to shake Sue's hand. "If this joker gives you any lip, you let me know! Us ladies gotta stick together!" She winked as she released Sue's hand, then gave Wayne a friendly shoulder brush as she moved past him, walking with just enough sway in her hips to accentuate her assets.

Wayne rolled his eyes in mock disgust. He knew Stacey was only joking but made a mental note to make sure Sue knew it. He went out of his way to make sure the cowgirls at The Big M were treated with respect. That didn't mean there wasn't plenty of typical 'cowboy humor' going back and forth between everyone that worked on the ranch and Stacey could dish it out as good as she could take it. But it was all in good fun and anyone who treated someone in a truly disrespectful manner was only given one warning to straighten out their act. A second offence was a fireable one.

"Sorry about yesterday. Sometimes things come up that need tending to. Couldn't be helped."

"No problem. I had a nice conversation with Jake." Sue looked towards the house. "Interesting man."

"That he is. And the best boss I ever had," Wayne stated matter-of-factly.

Even though they had spoken on the phone, Sue finally realized he did not have much of an accent, dispelling her silly assumption that all true cowboys sounded as though they were from deep in the heart of Texas.

Before she could inquire further about what made Jake such a great boss, Wayne continued. "I worked for the previous owner, when the ranch was much, much smaller. I don't mind sayin' that, to my way of thinkin', he was an idiot. Really didn't have a clue about ranchin'. He had been successful doin' something else, don't ask me what, and figured he could be a rancher and take it easy all day. Which he pretty much did. But his laziness kept him outta my hair so I was OK with it, until he started thinkin' he knew better than me. Now I've been doin' this kinda work all my life but there for a while, he just wouldn't listen to me. Finally, I had a chance to show him how somethin' he wanted done would cost him a bunch of money that he wouldn't ever get back and he backed off. After that, he let me run things my way and we started doin' pretty good, even if it wasn't much fun to work here with him around. Eventually, Jake came along and offered to buy it and I figured it was gonna be another situation where someone who had no business out here was gonna come in and try to tell me how things should be done and I almost left. But I decided to at least meet him. Glad I did! Something felt different about him from the moment I met him. Not the pretentious prick I expected. He told me right from the start he wanted to learn all he could from me and as long as the ranch was doin' OK, he'd leave me run it. And he has! But if it wasn't for him we'd never have grown to what we are today. Smart business people, Mary and him." Wayne realized he was talking about things Sue probably didn't care about. "Sorry, I'm going on and on and you haven't even asked your first question! Let's go over here and take a load off." He led her to benches that sat between the house and the main barn with a beautiful view of the corral and the meadow beyond. With the sun bright in the sky, the mild weather made sitting outside in the fresh air a welcome change from conducting interviews indoors.

"I really appreciate your time," Sue started. "You already know why I'm here so do you have any questions before we start or is there anything you want me to know?"

Wayne had one simple question. "I don't know much about travelin'. The little I've done is mostly to cattle auctions. And ridin' around this ranch doesn't count. You really think folks care about what we do at Christmas? Not sure it's all that special."

"I have a feeling you do some unique things for the holiday that I think people will enjoy knowing about. At least, that's my hope."

He rubbed his neck a bit, as was his habit when he was perplexed. "Well, OK, you're the expert. I'll do my best to help you out."

"Great. Before we get into your holiday traditions though, I'm curious what's the best thing about working here, living here, spending your holidays here? I'm assuming most cowboys don't get to leave their ranch for Christmas so what makes this place special enough for you that you want to spend it here?"

"You met him. Jake makes this place what it is, makes it special. You can probably imagine we work hard and if you stick around, you'll get to see just how hard. But Jake works even harder. When we got somethin' that needs doin', Jake is there, sweatin', diggin' in and getting' it done with the rest of us. That's not typical of ranch owners, least not the ones in my experience."

"After our conversation yesterday, I can tell he's different. Seems like the cowboy life can be very interesting. Can you tell me about how the cowboy themed vacations work?"

Wayne grinned. "Oh, they're a hoot! Usually starts with people comin' out here to get away from city life, thinkin' they got what it takes to live on a ranch. But as soon as they discover the cell service out here pretty much sucks, they start to panic at bein' cut off from everything they think is so important. They moan and complain and think they just can't handle it...until they start to relax. After a day or two, they figure out there is more to life than useless stuff like knowing what their friends are doing every minute of the day or getting riled up about stuff that don't affect them anyway."

"Well, I have to admit getting used to the lack of cell service out here has been a bit of any adjustment. But I'm actually starting to see the upside." Sue's phone hadn't rung once since arriving in Spruce and she was realizing she was glad of it.

"Exactly. So once people start adjustin' to that, we put 'em to work. Depending on the time of year, we might be branding cattle, movin' 'em to a different pasture, mending fences, cuttin' horses, whatever. We don't let 'em do anything where they might get hurt but they still help out and get involved. Some folks get right into the cowboy stuff but some aren't as adventurous so there is always plenty of ranch hand chores to do like milking cows, feeding the chickens and turkeys, brushing the horses, stuff like that. And some people just like to sit and watch and relax. Whatever folks want to do is fine with us."

Everything he described sounded like a delightful vacation to Sue. She was starting to think her next one would be right there! "Sounds like a vacation here is very different, but in a good way."

"Yeah, different but special. The fall and winter vacations are the best. The beauty of a snow covered field in the winter is something to see. And there is something about Thanksgiving and Christmas that is really special out here."

"Why is that?"

"They were Mary's favorite holidays. That's Jake late wife. She always made sure things were extra special for folks who were here for either of those holidays."

"Jake mentioned that the Thanksgiving celebrations are pretty popular."

Wayne let out a hearty chuckle. "That's putting it mildly! We get fifty guests each year and that ain't countin' the folks that come from town. There's a ton of great food and Betsy at the bakery makes the best fresh pumpkin pies you've ever tasted. We always have one heck of a good time!"

"Fifty guests! The house is big but it's not that big. Where does everyone stay?"

"When the rooms at the main house are all booked, we have some cabins on the ranch for families and some of the more adventurous guests will even camp out in the field beyond the corral. Then Jake puts the rest up in town. Hires a shuttle to get 'em back and forth. Pays all the extra costs himself. Says it's not right to charge people more just because he don't have space on the ranch for 'em."

Everything he was telling her seemed extraordinary to Sue. She had never heard of such an accommodating business. The expression on her face must have given her thoughts away as she was having trouble putting them into words.

Wayne understood completely. "People who have been comin' here for years really want to be here no matter what," he said with a wide grin. "And Jake loves havin' 'em. I think it's his favorite holiday."

"Do you have a favorite holiday?"

"Oh that's easy. The Fourth of July!"

Sue caught herself from blurting out her usual two-word question when she wasn't getting the details she needed. "Why the fourth?"

"It's really special. Mary passed from cancer so every July 4th, Jake invites a group of cancer patients to come out here for the week, breathe in the fresh air and relax a bit, take time off from dealing with cancer every day. He calls it the 'Independence from Cancer' vacation. And it does those folks a world of good. The mind can be a great healer. So many of those folks are rejuvenated while they're here. I've seen some arrive too weak to walk on their own and they leave walking without any help!"

"That's truly special."

"Yes ma'am. It's really important to Jake that people who have to deal with that terrible disease every day just get some time to...I don't know...forget about it for a bit, have some fun. He brings doctors and nurses out with the patients, in case someone takes a turn for the worse. I think they enjoy it as much as their patients. And Jake pays for it all himself."

"Jake pays for it!?" Sue was starting to think the owner of The Big M was too good to be true.

"I'm certain that a huge expense."

"I guess. But I also guess he can afford it. It's real important to him."

She scribbled some notes before continuing. "And what about Christmas? What special things happen for that holiday? After all, that's what I'm here to find out!"

Wayne smiled as he winked at Sue. "Well now, you'll just have to stick around and see. Come with me to the barn and I'll introduce you around so you can get the stuff you need. But to really know what we do, you'll have to experience Christmas at The Big M!"

If I only had that much time she thought as she followed Wayne. The Big M seemed like the perfect place to celebrate the holiday. But with a looming deadline, she didn't have the luxury of experiencing Christmas at The Big M. At least, not this year.

CHAPTER 8

As Sue prepared to go downstairs and have a late morning breakfast at the inn, her phone rang. Checking the name of the caller made her realize she hadn't talked to Melanie for several days! "Hey there."

"Hey there yourself! Where have you been? I haven't heard from you in days!" Melanie's scolding words spilled forth without pause.

"Sorry, I've been busy trying to wrangle cowboys."

"I'll bet!" Her sarcasm seeped through the phone.

"Oh stop! And the cell service out here is less-than-stellar. The only reason you got through to me now is because I'm connected to the inn's wi-fi."

"Well, thankfully you aren't dead in a ditch somewhere!"

Sue giggled. "Don't be so dramatic."

"How's the research going?"

"OK so far but I really need to do more interviews, find out more unique things they do. And I'm hoping to *see* some of the things they do so I'll probably be staying a bit longer than I originally planned."

"In other words, you're telling me you won't be able to help me find a tree this year."

Sue could hear her friend's disappointment. They both enjoyed their yearly tradition of shopping for the perfect tree. "Do you hate me?"

"Don't be ridiculous! I can handle it this year. You've trained me well."

"Glad you have the situation under control. And don't worry if you don't hear from me. I'm finding more to this town than I expected and I plan to learn all about it so I can include it in the article. I'm meeting lots of genuinely nice people."

Melanie heard something different in her friend's voice. Something good. "Just be sure you're back by Christmas Eve. That's a holiday tradition you aren't allowed to miss!"

"Understood! I'll call you soon." Sue smiled as she ended the call. Even though she wanted to be with her friend, she really was happy to be in Spruce and was looking forward to learning more about it, the Big M Ranch and....Jake.

*****

"Zac, thanks so much for accommodating my late start this morning with such a tasty breakfast." He was clearing away Sue's plate in what was otherwise an empty dining room.

"No problem! We always try to accommodate our guest's schedules!" He liked Sue. And while he knew she wasn't there to write about the inn, he held out hope that she would at least mention Holiday House in her article.

She smiled in appreciation. "And I have to ask. The strawberry tart, where did those come from?"

"Right from our own kitchen." Zac beamed with pride, realizing the tarts might be just the thing to get the inn mentioned in the article. "My wife Mia makes them."

"Well, I have to tell you, I've spent a lot of time in Scotland and I've never tasted a Strawberry Tart in the US that can hold a candle to the ones I get there." Now it all made sense to Sue. "But since your wife is Scottish, I can see she brought the tradition over with her."

Zac gave her a devilish grin. "It's what she missed the most from home so she wanted to feature them at the inn. They make us a bit unique and also provide her a fond memory from her childhood."

"Does she make a lot of traditional Scottish dishes?"

He let out a hearty laugh. "Sorry, don't mean any disrespect but she can barely cook anything other than Strawberry Tarts. In fact, she hates cooking. I do it all. But she was determined to make tarts that tasted the same as what she used to get at a place called The Kandy Bar. It took her months to perfect the recipe. I went to Scotland with her one time and tried the tarts she emulated. And I gotta say, she got it right!"

Sue smiled at the memory of her travels to the beautiful land of sheep, kilts, highlands and whiskey. It was probably her favorite country to visit in Europe so she appreciated what Mia had accomplished in learning to make tarts the way her favorite pastry shop did. "Zac, would you have a few minutes to talk to me about the inn and maybe provide some background on The Big M ranch?"

He looked around the empty dining room with a wry smile. "I think I can spare as many minutes as you need." He refilled

Sue's coffee and filled a mug for himself, then sat down at the table. "What can I tell you?"

For half an hour, Sue learned the history of the inn, how it started as a boarding house in the mid-to-late 1800's, became a makeshift hospital in the early 1900's when a fever spread through the region and eventually became an orphanage. It fell into disrepair and sat unused for years until Zac and Mia bought it after tiring of living in Chicago and being overworked by the company where they were employed for years. "Even though we were making a very good living, we weren't satisfied. We wanted something better for ourselves." Both of them had long dreamed of having a business of their own and bought the building, restored it and opened "the finest inn in all of Spruce," Zac proclaimed proudly, knowing he didn't have much competition.

Eventually, the conversation turned to Jake and his ranch. Zac and Mia came to town not long after Jake and Mary. He felt Jake had an interesting story to tell but he never really gave a lot of details about where they came from or what they did before arriving at The Big M. Everyone in town assumed Jake and Mary had always been ranchers but Zac sensed differently. He never pushed them for details though, figuring *if he wants to tell me about his past, he'll do it. Otherwise, it's none of my business.* "I'll tell you one thing. Jake is someone who cares about people, about the community. Last year, when the church's organ broke, he brought in a specialist from back east to repair it since it was so old no one else knew what to do with it. He knows the church is the center of a lot of community activities and he wanted to make sure the music didn't die!"

"Interesting that he had that connection," Sue mused. "From everything I'm hearing so far, he sounds like a unique individual."

"That he is. Like I said, he cares. He sponsors the substance abuse group meetings held at the church. The program is real important to him, almost personal. But it's important to a lot of people. My best friend's son realized he needed that kind of help a few years ago and when Jake found out he had to drive to meetings that were thirty miles away, he did what needed to be done to start a group here in town. Paid for everything to be set up and continues to cover most of the expenses. For that program alone, the town owes Jake a lot."

The more Zac talked, the more Sue was intrigued by the town and the ranch. If not for Mark's suggestion, she would not have found everything she had stumbled upon. She made a mental note to thank him with a batch of her special chocolate chip cookies upon her return! "Thank you so much for your time and all this information Zac. It's really quite enlightening."

"Happy to help. You let me know if you need anything else. In the meantime, I'll tell Mia to make sure she keeps you stocked in tarts!"

Sue smiled as they both got up and he finished clearing the table. "I promise they won't go to waste! See you later." As she made her way back to her room, she was starting to get the sense there was more to Jake than she might have expected.

*****

Sue sat by the fireplace in her room enjoying the dancing flames, although she had to open the window to let some of the heat escape. Even with the mild weather, she couldn't resist the charm of having the fire on while she worked.

Having spent most of the previous day talking to cowboys and cowgirls about their Christmas traditions, she had plenty of notes to go through as she started to write the first draft of her article. She still needed the 'hook' that would make the article special though. So far, it seemed that everything each of them did for the holiday was interesting but not quite unique enough to satisfy her needs. So while she definitely needed something special and heartwarming to explore, she wasn't worried she wouldn't find it. Wayne had told her she'd have time to talk to as many cowpokes as she wanted over the next few days. And, she was planning to talk with JoAnne to gather more background on the town and, hopefully, The Big M.

As Sue worked through her notes, the phone next to the bed rang. She looked at it in amazement. *When was the last time I answered a land-line? And who knows I'm here?* She hadn't even told Melanie and Jackie where she was staying. She picked up the receiver. "Hello?"

"Hey there. It's Wayne."

"Hey there yourself! How did you know where to find me?"

"I have my sources. Besides, there are only a few places in town that I figured would be up to the standards of a world-traveler like yourself. Zac was my first call."

"Are all cowboys as resourceful as you?"

"Only the good ones," he responded with a laugh. "If a cowboy ain't resourceful, he ain't successful."

"I'm going to quote you on that!"

"Feel free. But for now, I need you to put on some comfortable clothes and come out to the ranch as soon as you can. And bring a warm coat. The temperature is going to dip later."

"And what am I coming there to do?"

"Can't tell you that. It'll ruin the surprise."

She was intrigued. "I'd love to but I really need to get some work done."

Wayne was insistent. "Trust me, this is research for your story. You want to know about cowboy Christmas traditions, right?"

"Of course."

"Then we'll see you in an hour."

Sue could envision the clever smile on Wayne's face as he hung up the phone without another word. While she did have work to do, she didn't think that Wayne would waste her time. And having just read her notes, she knew that more research was needed if she was going to turn in the strong article she needed. So she quickly changed into comfortable clothing that should work for whatever Wayne had planned and grabbed her coat as she left the room.

Making her way down to the lobby, Sue's imagination started to run wild with what was in store for her at the ranch. She hoped it had something to do with spending time with horses so on her way through the lobby, she spied a bowl of fruit and grabbed an apple, just in case.

*****

In less than an hour from talking with Wayne, Sue drove through the entrance to The Big M ranch. As she pulled up to the barn area it was easy to see something was in the works. A large, weathered but sturdy looking wagon was being hitched to a couple of horses while others were being saddled. Jake was talking with Wayne and both seemed to be directing what was happening as Bernie was doing his best to get underfoot of everyone, playing a game only a dog could understand. She parked and walked over to the group.

Wayne was glad Jake liked his idea to invite Sue. "Just in time!"

"Just in time for what?"

"Wayne here decided you should take part in our annual Christmas tree hunt."

"Christmas tree hunt?" Sue was perplexed...and intrigued. "Could you provide some additional details please?

Jake was excited to explain. "I imagine that you are someone who likes a fresh tree each Christmas. No artificial tree for you, right?"

"Absolutely....if I had room for one. My apartment is pretty small. But I help my friend Melanie find the perfect tree for her condo every year. We make shopping for it an event."

"You mean 'hunting' for it. I imagine you hit several tree lots each year."

Sue smiled.

"So, it's a hunt! And cowboys do the same. And right now, it's time for our annual Cowboy Christmas Tree Hunt. Except we don't go to tree lots. We go right to the source. And that's where we're heading now."

"You mean you have Christmas trees on the ranch?" Jake appeared to be more into Christmas than she expected.

"Sure do. There was a section of various spruce trees on the ranch when I bought it so I trim them up every year. We've been getting some beauties for years now. This year will be no exception. But we need a woman's eye to find just the right ones."

Stacey happened to be within earshot. "Again, what am I here for? To shovel horseshit?!"

Wayne threw her a look. "You ain't done that since you were officially branded a cowgirl."

"Damn right!" she snapped back with a wide grin.

The horrified look on Sue's face as she imagined a brand being burned into Stacey's rear end made Wayne burst out laughing. "Don't worry, it's just a figure of speech." He threw her a wink as he got back to work saddling a horse. "We stopped actually branding cowpokes years ago."

A relived Sue laughed as she turned back to Jake. "Did you say 'ones'?"

Wayne interjected. "Jake isn't the only one that wants a tree. The bunkhouses need some holiday cheer!"

Sue looked at Jake. "I wondered why there was no tree in the main house."

"Haven't had time until today. And this will be your first experience actually doing a 'cowboy Christmas tradition'."

"Other cowboys do this?"

"The ones who like Christmas do," he replied with a broad grin that told Sue he was looking forward to 'the hunt'.

With the preparations winding down, everyone was seemingly ready to go. "Am I riding in the wagon?" Sue inquired, trying not to give away her disappointment if that was their plan.

"If you're up for it, I've saddled that horse over there for you." Wayne pointed to a large and beautiful Appaloosa tied to the fence as he laughed to himself, playing a good-natured joke on Sue knowing someone unfamiliar with horse riding would be intimidated by one the size of Lucy. He wanted to see how long Sue would go along before he revealed that the smaller horse he had just finished saddling was the one he actually intended her to ride, if she was game.

Jake hoped Sue had a sense of humor or he'd be in trouble as he played along and assured her. "We'll help you mount and dismount. Riding her will be more comfortable than being in the wagon." He winked at Wayne.

Sue had been waiting for this moment. She walked over to Lucy and untied the reins. She gently put her hand on Lucy's long snout and ran her fingers up and down. Lucy's ear twitched as Sue put her mouth to it and whispered while her other hand moved to the horse's neck. Wayne and Jake gave each other curious glances. As Sue continued to gently whisper to Lucy, she reached into her pocket to retrieve the apple and held it to Lucy's mouth. As it was eagerly consumed, Sue patted Lucy's neck, then swiftly moved to the horse's side and expertly mounted the noble beast as though she had done so a thousand times.

Settling in the saddle, she looked at Jake and the others, whose mouths were agape. *Guess they weren't expecting me to do that.* "Not my first time at the rodeo."

Stacey broke the deafening silence with roaring laughter. "You idiots act like you never seen a woman saddle-up before!"

Wayne quickly realized he had severely underestimated Sue while everyone applauded. He finally gathered himself enough to speak. "Actually, that's my horse. I just told you she was yours as a joke. This one is really for you."

Very satisfied that she ruined Wayne's joke, Sue turned the good-natured ribbing back on him. "Looks like the joke is on you," she stated with a smile. "You get the small horse today."

She looked around before he could protest and inquired, "Now, who is leading this hunt?" as she expertly brought Lucy around and pointed her in the direction of the meadow. Stacey looked at her and gave her a respectful nod.

Jake and everyone else realized how silly they looked and quickly got themselves organized. With everything they needed in the wagon, they were ready to go as Jake looked at Sue sitting confidently on Wayne's horse. "Right this way ma'am!" Bernie saw the party was finally on the move and scrambled to jump into the wagon, determined not to miss out on the fun. The tree hunt was on as Jake led the way to the grove where the perfect ones awaited.

*****

The hunting party took it's time getting to their destination, which was fine with Sue. It felt good being on a horse again and she wanted it to last as long as possible. Wayne had taken over leading the party as Jake hung back to talk with her.

"It suits you, sitting on that horse. But you coulda knocked me over with a swipe of its tail when I saw you mount up!"

"Feels good to ride again."

Jake could clearly tell there was more to Sue than he imagined. "So how is it a city girl knows about horse flesh?"

"I love horses. I love animals! I took some riding lessons when I was young."

"I think you took more than 'some' lessons." He knew from experience no one saddled up that smoothly and rode as well as she was without a lot of training. "I think you've been holding out on me."

She became bashful. "Well, if you must know, I was a top five finalist in the Little Britches Rodeo National finals when I was twelve years old." She smiled as she fondly recalled her youthful dreams. "Told my parents I was going to be the first cowgirl in our family."

"Impressive. You don't get far in that competition without knowing what you're doing. Why didn't you mention it the other day? I would think you'd want to ride a horse while you're here."

"To be honest, I wasn't sure I could still get into the saddle without embarrassing myself."

He let out a laugh. "Yeah, I don't think I would have let you live it down if you fell off while getting on!"

"But once I saw this beauty with her calm eyes, it all came rushing back to me." Sue gave Lucy a loving pat on her strong neck. "And before I knew it, I was in the saddle and, thankfully, stayed there!"

"So how did aspirations of being a cowgirl turn into being a writer?"

She tried to hide her regret as she looked straight before giving a reply to his innocent inquiry. "I wasn't sure I had what it took to do what everyone on this ranch does every day. I loved riding so much but..." She paused, then shrugged. "I knew that wasn't enough. But I knew I had what it took to be a writer."

Jake wanted to know more but sensed the sadness she was trying to hide and stopped himself from exploring further. But there was definitely something more to the person whom he had met on the side of the road only days earlier. Had being on the ranch awakened something in her? She most certainly knew how to ride and she seemed like she was capable and smart enough to accomplish anything she set her mind to. It had been a long time since he had met a woman like Sue and hoped there would be another opportunity to learn more about her.

Sue was thankful they rode on in silence and after another 20 minutes, they were approaching the tree farm as Jake moved to the front of the group. When they arrived at the farm's edge, they stopped and dismounted. Axes, saws and ropes were retrieved from the wagon as Bernie jumped down and everyone set out on foot with a couple men staying behind to mind the horses, who were happy to graze on grass not yet covered in snow.

Sue and Jake along with Stacey and Wayne started to inspect the trees while Bernie sniffed everything in sight, seemingly having found the scent of an animal he was intent on finding. Sue was surprised to find so many perfect trees in one place. She looked at every tree, having a hard time determining which one was the best, which was unusual for her since she had a keen eye for Christmas trees. That's why Melanie insisted Sue help her find one every year!

"Jake, you must spend a lot of time out here pruning these. I know enough about spruce trees to know they don't grow this full and perfectly shaped naturally."

"It's a favorite pastime of mine. I stared pruning them when the kids were little, figuring it would be a nice family outing every year to pick out and cut down our tree."

Jake has kids! Sue was surprised he hadn't mentioned them before now. But then, why would he? She wasn't doing an article on him. Still, she wanted to know more about him but sensed maybe it would be best to wait until later to ask about his family.

And Jake was thankful she didn't ask anything further since he was sorry he had brought up his kids at all. He didn't want to ruin the afternoon by talking about them.

They continued to search through the trees until Sue turned and saw it! A beautiful tall blue spruce with branches that were full and strong. She excitedly looked at every side of the tree and couldn't decide which was more perfect. "Here it is, the perfect tree," she exclaimed!

Jake followed the sound of her voice and soon stood next to her admiring the tree she claimed to be 'the one'. "She's a beauty. And tall. Think it'll fit?"

"Are you kidding? This tree will look beautiful in front of the window in your great room. It'll be absolutely perfect!" She was having a hard time containing her excitement.

"I usually put the tree next to the fireplace," Jake replied wistfully as he recalled Mary declaring it to be the perfect spot for the tree every year.

Sue quickly ascertained there were certain holiday traditions that Jake likely still followed years after losing his wife, as he should, and she realized she might be stepping on hollowed territory with her proclamation. "Sorry. I don't mean to tell you how to decorate your own house. You certainly know what you like and obviously it'll look just as grand next to the fireplace, ready to greet Santa as he comes down the chimney!" She hoped her silly attempt to lighten the mood would work.

Thankfully it did as his mood brightened a bit. "Well, regardless of where it's placed, you are the Christmas tree expert so if you say this is the one, then this one it shall be." He grabbed a saw from one of the men and started cutting the tree about a foot up from the ground. "Timber," he yelled in warning as the tree gently fell. Without snow on the ground, they couldn't drag it without ruining it so a couple of the men grabbed the tree and carried it to the wagon as Jake retrieved a short length of thin rope from his pocket. With about a foot of the tree stump sticking up from the ground, he spotted the sturdiest branch on the stump just below where he made the cut. He worked the rope under the branch and gently pulled it upright, tying the rope around the trunk so that the branch stood straight up. Sue watched him complete the task before asking why he did it. "When you cut a tree, if you tie a strong branch upright like I just did, the tree will regrow." Sue gave him a look that told him she was certain he was pulling her leg. He put his right hand up. "I swear it's true. Learned it from my dad. Come back in ten years and we'll be able to cut down the same tree again!"

Suddenly, Jake felt awkward. So did Sue. They looked at each other for a moment before Stacey thankfully shouted. "Hey Sue, come here and tell these knuckleheads the tree I found is perfect for their smelly bunkhouse!" Sue blushed and quickly turned to walk towards Stacey's voice with her thoughts running wild and Bernie on her heels.

*****

With their bounty of perfect trees nestled securely in the wagon, the hunt was complete and the party started their return. Wayne was game enough to let Sue continue to ride Lucy on the trip back to the house even though she volunteered to switch horses with him. Bernie was happy to jump into the wagon to avoid the long walk home and everyone was satisfied with the results of the journey.

The trip back to the house was quieter than when they had started the hunt just a few hours prior. Sue hoped that her declaration of where Jake's tree should be placed didn't somehow ruin the day. It had been a fun experience and she appreciated that she was made part of it. She wanted to know more about Jake but now clearly was not the time.

Arriving at the house just before dusk, short work was made of getting the trees out of the wagon and into tree stands that had been cleaned and prepared by Dolly while the hunting party was out seeking its "prey". Sue had only spoken to Dolly briefly but was certain she was key to the smooth operation of the ranch. She had apparently been with Jake for quite some time so Sue was hoping to have more time for them to speak soon since during their only conversation, Dolly had very matter-of-factly told her Jake couldn't manage without her and Sue believed it. From what she could see, Dolly was always prepared with hot food, sound advice and an 'I won't put up with any of your nonsense' attitude! Her short and stocky stature helped to emphasize that no BS attitude. But she seemed like a level-headed, good-natured person and thankfully had also prepared particularly tasty hot chocolate for the returning hunters who cheerfully related the story of how Sue had dumfounded Wayne when she mounted his horse like an expert. To which Wayne quickly defended his reaction by pointing out they were *all* dumbfounded! Preparing the trees and relating the stories of the day seemed to perk up Jake as he stood admiring the tree they had cut for his house.

Dolly eyed the tree as it stood in its stand. "Are you sure this thing will fit in the house? Looks taller than normal."

Jake gave a knowing nod. "It'll fit. Come on boys. Let's get this monster into place!"

Cowboy Bill and James, a quiet cowboy Sue hadn't gotten to talk with much, made quick work of carrying the tree up to Jake's house while Dolly went ahead to make sure the path through the great room was clear. As she moved a small table from the area next to the fireplace where the tree was traditionally placed, an action she had done for many years, Jake stopped her. "I'm thinking the tree should go in front of the bay window this year Dolly. What do you think?"

She was, quite simply, shocked. She had never known Jake to deviate from the traditions that had been set up years ago, mostly by Mary. She had always figured he kept the traditions alive to honor his wife and wasn't sure how to respond to his statement. "But...the tree has always been placed in this corner. Its tradition."

"Indeed, it has been the tradition for years. But maybe it's time for a change, time for a new tradition." Oddly enough, he had been feeling ready for a change. "With the tree in front of the window, it can be appreciated from inside and outside the house. It suddenly seems like the perfect spot."

His satisfied smile told Dolly his mind was set. "Well, it's certainly tall enough to fill the space in that 20 foot window!" Dolly suddenly went from not wanting to break tradition to getting the change completed in the most efficient manner. "But we'll need the men to move those chairs so the tree can be centered." Bernie sensed there was too much going on for him to do anything but curl up in his bed and watch as Cowboy Bill and James were quick to do as Dolly instructed. With the chairs out of the way, the tree was placed in the center of the window, just as Sue had suggested.

"Perfect," Dolly proclaimed. Then the cowboys were off to get the other trees placed while Dolly went to get water to fill the tree stand.

Sue gazed at the tree. Even without decorations it was grand and beautiful in the spot she had suggested. But she couldn't help feeling she had somehow forced Jake into making a change that he might not have been prepared for. Not that she had pushed the idea. She simply made an assumption that now seemed to be well beyond the bounds for someone so new to the group.

"Looks great, doesn't it?" Jake was standing next to the fireplace, where the tree was traditionally placed, staring at its new home.

"I think it does. But please tell me you didn't put it here because I suggested it," she pleaded.

"I absolutely did put it there because you suggested it!" He firmly stated. "And I also did it because it's a great idea. I don't know why I didn't think of it sooner!"

Sue stared at him for a moment, not sure she completely believed him. He was obviously devoted to his wife and tried to keep her memory alive, which she respected, and she didn't know him well enough to even think of suggesting he change anything that Mary had started. She made a mental note to stay in her place. And decided it was time for a new conversation topic! "I really enjoyed today. Thanks very much for inviting me to experience my first Cowboy Christmas Tradition!"

Jake became sheepish. "So, I may have exaggerated a bit when I told you the tree hunt is a real Cowboy Christmas Tradition. But it's a favorite one around here."

Sue contemplated what he told her for a moment. She felt it necessary to figure out a way to work the hunt into her article.

"Let me ask you this. Were we out there hunting for trees with real cowboys?"

"Yes." He wasn't sure where this was headed.

"And the hunt is a tradition you do every year?"

"Yes." He smiled as he started to catch on.

"Then as far as I'm concerned, it qualifies as a Cowboy Christmas Tradition!" she proclaimed.

"I like you're way of thinking! But with a tree this size, I'm gonna need some help decorating it. You game?"

She eagerly agreed since it was starting to look as though this might be the only tree she would get to decorate this year. Dolly had already placed the boxes of decorations in the room so Jake untangled the lights as Sue started to look through the tree ornaments. Many of the beautiful decorations appeared to be carefully hand crafted. "These are gorgeous! Did Mary make them?"

"Yes, she was talented like that. She made most of them but some were made by guests. Mary would have an ornament making workshop with the guests every year. A lot of them picked up the helpful hints she gave them pretty quickly and made some really nice ornaments for us."

"Did your kids make any of these?"

"No, they didn't get into that stuff."

"That's a shame. I remember making ornaments with my parents each year. It's one of my fondest memories of time with my parents."

"Will you be spending Christmas with them?"

Sue paused for a moment. "They passed away when I was in college." She didn't want to dampen the conversation with the details of her parents demise but she didn't feel it made sense to avoid their deaths altogether.

"I'm very sorry." Jake suddenly realized he knew very little about Sue. "Losing family is a painful thing."

"That it is." Their conversation paused for several moments while each tried to think of something cheerful to talk about. Sue was the first to speak up. "So did your kids at least join in the Cowboy Christmas Tree Hunt each year?" *Everyone likes talking about their kids* she thought!

"Never. Even though I worked on the trees for them, thinking it was something we could enjoy together, by the time the trees were ready for cutting, they weren't interested and then when Mary got sick..." Jake's voice trailed off. "They just never took part in the hunt."

Good job Sue! Obviously his kids are not a cheerful topic. The conversation was continuing to go south at a rapid pace! They decorated in silence for several minutes before Sue got her phone out and opened a Christmas music playlist that consisted mostly of upbeat tunes sure to liven up any situation. At least, that was her hope. As the music played, Jake started to hum along and before they knew it, they were both singing along. Sue was surprised at how many of the songs Jake knew and when *Christmas For Cowboys* came on, she was treated to Jake's surprisingly strong baritone voice singing every lyric. "That's not a well-known song!" she exclaimed when the music finished. "I'm impressed you know it."

"It's a personal favorite of mine." She looked at him with a surprised expression. "Think about it. It's a song about cowboys at Christmas. How can I not like it?! I have all of John Denver's albums. Love his stuff."

Jake was quickly becoming a most interesting person to Sue. The reporter in her couldn't help but want to know more about what happened with his kids but she had almost derailed the day twice by bringing them up. She wasn't about to press for more details.

They continued to decorate as Dolly appeared with thick sandwiches of tender sliced turkey, kettle chips and pickle slices that would make the best deli jealous. "You two need to eat!" she commanded. Realizing they were famished, they both took a break to enjoy the food. But it wasn't long before they were back at the decorating, having noticed bare spots that needed an ornament as they admired the tree while eating.

Finally, the food and tree were finished. They stood back and admired their handiwork. Sue thought Jake had done a marvelous job of spacing the lights while she managed to hang ornaments in every open space. Now it was time for the star to be placed and top off their efforts. Jake held onto Sue as she climbed the step ladder to get the star perfectly placed. He hadn't held a woman on a ladder since Mary had been well enough to place the star. *Was it finally time for new traditions?*

He looked at Sue as she got down from the ladder, appreciating her willingness to try new things and admiring her sense of adventure. He hadn't met a woman like her since....Mary. Shaking off the thoughts that were invading his head, he looked at the tree as he spoke. "Thank you for being here today...and for helping with everything...all this." He was having trouble expressing his thoughts, like a shy school boy. "I really enjoyed today."

She sensed confusion in him and wanted to say the right thing but could only manage "I've enjoyed this as well. Thank you."

An awkward silence passed between them, then Jake snapped back to himself. "Can I interest you in a hot, spiked apple cider for all your efforts? You've certainly earned it!"

"Now that sounds like the perfect way to cap off the perfect day." The glee Jake sensed in her voice was genuine. She wasn't certain of the last time she enjoyed a day so much. Riding a horse, hunting for a tree, decorating that tree, the company she was in...it all made for a perfect day.

Jake knew by the aroma wafting from the kitchen that Dolly had left mulled cider simmering for them. As Sue followed him into the large, well-equipped kitchen, he took two mugs from the wall and ladled the steaming liquid into both, then motioned for her to follow him. They walked through the dining room which held a live-edge thick wooden table large enough to seat at least twenty people comfortably to a wall of windows with French doors in the middle. Passing through the doors onto a large stone patio, there were several chairs placed around a fire pit which was prepared with kindling and an impressive wood pile, ready to provide warmth against an evening that had turned seasonably cold. Jake started the fire as Sue sat in one of the chairs close to the rim of the pit. Once the fire was burning strong, he sat in the chair next to her. They sipped on the cider as they watched the dancing flames. As a slight breeze started to blow, Sue was beginning to really appreciate the warmth being provided by both the fire and the cider.

"So, I'm no expert but aren't most articles about Christmas already published this close to the day?" Jake had been wanting to ask the question for a while.

"Excellent observation!" Sue explained how her annual Christmas article always arrived in two parts with this year's first part, covering the traditions of police, firemen, doctors, etc., having been printed in the December issue on newsstands and that the second part, about the traditions of cowboys, would be put up on the magazine's website a few days before Christmas.

Jake took all the information in with great interest, asking a few questions during the discussion that Sue thought were very intuitive, especially for someone who probably had never given any thought to the type of work she did. Finally he asked, "So how is the "cowboy" part coming?"

"Slow. I keep getting sidetracked," she playfully chided him.

"Blame Wayne for today. It was his idea!"

She stared at the fire and smiled. "I'll be certain to thank him tomorrow. But I do need a few more traditions like what we did today."

"Well, that's a bit of a problem."

"Oh, don't tell me there is some secret oath all cowboys take to never reveal what they do at Christmas!" she teased.

He enjoyed her playfulness. "No, nothing as serious as that," he replied with a chuckle. "We save the secret oaths for important stuff like not revealing the proper way to cook beans in a can on an open fire pit!"

"Thank goodness. No way I can come up with a new topic this late in the game!"

"Pretty sure you don't need to do that. But I'm not sure you can easily lump all cowboys into one group, thinking of all of us doing the same things at Christmas. At least not enough that will fill an article like you've described. After all, just because cowboys have the same basic job it doesn't mean they all have the same holiday traditions. I'm thinking your readers want to know about things they can experience, things they can relate to or envision. But some of the stuff cowboys do is unique to the setting or person and might not really be of interest to everyone."

Being both concerned for her article and intrigued by his comments, Sue asked for further elaboration.

"Think back to the first part of your article. I'm pretty sure that police in Boston have different traditions than police in Bozeman, Montana, even though they all do the same job. Military families, doctors, firefighters... I'm thinking they all have different ways of celebrating the holiday that are influenced by where they live or their background and aren't necessarily related to their professions." Jake got up to put more wood on the fire, stirring the coals before placing the logs.

"You may be onto something. It's true that I had a more difficult time than I expected finding similar traditions in the professions I researched. But I managed to find enough to string together an article, which ended up being as much about appreciating the work people do who aren't in 9 to 5 jobs as much as it was about appreciating the ways they celebrate Christmas. But their holiday traditions are still very important to them."

"Sounds about right."

"But I can't help feeling there might be certain things that are unique to most cowboys that will be intriguing to my readers and they might appreciate knowing some of the things that bond cowboys together at this time of year. Maybe show them that we all have things in common even though sometimes they are hard to recognize." Sue was again starting to doubt the validity of her subject choice. "I'm hoping that cowboys are intriguing to people partly because they don't know much about them."

"I think I understand what you're after but cowboys mostly enjoy a simple life and don't really feel the need to take part in holiday parties or exchanging gifts, etc."

"Maybe it's not something they do but something they experience as part of what they do for a living."

"Well, if they're lucky enough to be tending the herd on Christmas, out on the range, surrounded by the beauty of nature on a peaceful night, staring at the campfire, listening to the music the wind plays as it blows through the trees...." He paused as he watched the fire and shook his head slightly. "There's just no better celebration than to have time to reflect on the real meaning of the season, the birth of Jesus and the offer of peace he brought to us. Some folks experience that peace more than others but it's there if people choose to recognize it." Not wanting to make the conversation too serious, Jake stopped talking as they listened for several moments before he interrupted the sound of the breeze in the trees. "But I'll tell you one thing every cowboy on the range has more of than any folks in the city at Christmas."

Sue was intrigued. "What's that?"

He pointed up to the night sky as he replied. "Christmas lights!"

She looked up to see a star-filled sky like she had never experienced before. Millions of stars sparkled in the clear night sky like twinkling lights on a Christmas tree. She hadn't seen a sky this beautiful since...ever. Her amazement and appreciation of the beauty above her was apparent as the sight of the sky took her breath away.

"And on Christmas," Jake continued, "the stars shine just a little bit brighter!"

Sue was certain he was right as she stored his words in her memory. The perfect day had turned into a perfect evening and she didn't want it to end. And even though she knew it soon would, she didn't feel sad as the peacefulness of the moment seeped deep into her soul.

CHAPTER 9

Sue became aware that the sun was up as she snuck a peek from under the cozy flannel sheets. She was also aware that she had awakened refreshed and...relaxed for the first time in a long while! Everything that had made up the Christmas Tree Hunt had been exhilarating and exhausting at the same time. And finally she had details of a specific 'Cowboy Christmas Tradition' so once she returned to the inn, she stayed up late working on her article before she forgot all she wanted to write. Now, after another restful sleep, she lazily lay in bed, snuggled under the down comforter and flannel sheets, resisting all thoughts of getting out of bed. She was relaxed and calm and content and wondered when she had last felt these feelings. Then she contemplated why they were present now. Was it the fact she had been able to spend time riding again? Was it the clean country air? The genuinely friendly people she met at every turn? Or was it something else? As she considered all the possibilities she glanced at the clock on her bedside table. 10:00! *How did I sleep so late?!* Realizing she was famished, she grudgingly got out of the warm bed and prepared for the day. As she was dressing, she decided that it would be a good day to talk to JoAnne.

"Good morning Sue!" Zac was cleaning up the dining area after the final guests had finished their breakfast as she came through on her way out.

"Morning Zac. What's the weather like today?" Even though she hadn't been at the inn very long, she quickly learned that Zac had an uncanny knack for weather stats and predictions that were amazingly accurate.

"It finally got below freezing last night. I think we're in for the cold weather we've been lucky enough to avoid so far."

Zac's news made Sue smile. "So I *will* get to wear the warm clothes I brought! I was beginning to think I should have packed for a trip to Florida."

"It's been mild but I promise you it won't stay that way. Anyone who's been praying for cold weather is gonna regret it real soon!"

"I'll be ready," she assured him. "Do you know if JoAnne is working at the diner this morning? I was thinking of heading over there for breakfast."

"She wasn't here so she better be there!" Zac tried to sound irritated that his sister hadn't helped with breakfast at the inn since it was at capacity but Sue could clearly see he was joking. She enjoyed Zac's dry sense of humor and she liked his wife's even more. From her travels, she knew that Scottish people had a sarcastic sense of humor and she laughed when Zac explained his frustration at the fact that it was sometimes hard for him to tell when his wife was joking or was actually irritated.

"Thanks Zac. I'll tell her you didn't even notice she wasn't here this morning." She heard Zac's hearty laughter as she walked out the front door. He was right. There was a bite to the air and it was noticeably colder than it had been the entire time she'd been in town. In fact, it had been so mild it had been difficult for Sue to get into the Christmas mood. But the cold temperature was sure to help with that and a brisk walk to the diner in the fresh air was just what she wanted at the moment.

As she walked down Main Street, Sue enjoyed greeting and being greeted by everyone she passed. Every time she had walked through town, total strangers had friendly greetings for seemingly everyone they met. This wasn't particularly unusual for the small towns she had visited over the years but she thought something was different in Spruce. People genuinely seemed satisfied here. She wondered why it was so different and made a note to ask Joanne her thoughts on the subject.

Sue felt like she was actually starving when she walked through the door of the diner. JoAnne greeted her warmly as soon as she arrived and led the way to an empty table. *Sleigh Ride* by Andy Williams was providing a cheery atmosphere as JoAnne poured coffee with a broad smile on her face. "Do you know what you want?"

"What's the best breakfast item on the menu? I'm starving and I want something sweet and delicious!"

"You gotta try the pecan pancakes! Charlie roasts the pecans before putting them in the batter to open up the flavor. And they're served with warm homemade pecan syrup. Delish!"

"You haven't steered me wrong yet! Pecan pancakes it is, with a side of crispy bacon please."

"Comin' right up!" JoAnne was barking the order to Charlie before she got back to the counter while Sue was lost in thought, enjoying Elton John's *Step Into Christmas* as it came over the diner's speakers. She watched people as they walked past the window and hummed along with the music.

In what seemed like only minutes, JoAnne appeared with a plate of fresh pancakes and bacon that was crisped to perfection. "I'm really glad you stopped in today. I get off in about 15 minutes. Can I interest you in a cup of coffee at the bakery around the corner? Everything there is amazing and I'd love to pick your brain about traveling."

Sue could see the enthusiasm she held for learning about travel. "That sounds like the perfect way to cap off this delicious looking breakfast!" As JoAnne ran off to finish up her shift, Sue dug in to the steaming plate of food in front of her. Charlie knew what he was doing! The pancakes were moist and fluffy with a generous portion of nuts both inside and on top. And the bacon crumbled in her mouth just the way she liked. It wasn't easy to get bacon crispy without burning it but Charlie managed it and in the process, reminded Sue of how her perfectly her mother used to make it.

*****

"Thanks for the recommendation! Those pancakes were delicious! And the bacon was perfect." They were on their way to the coffee shop and Sue was grateful for the exercise. She wasn't sure she had room for anything else but JoAnne had promised her the bakery would be unforgettable.

"A diner without a good breakfast isn't a real diner!"

"Let me ask you something. I see some boarded up storefronts throughout town yet everyone seems so happy and content. Is the town struggling or are there just too many store fronts?"

"Both." JoAnne replied with a touch of sadness. "We were thriving for many years before the biggest employer in town moved their manufacturing to China. So, a good portion of the people here lost their jobs and businesses started to fail. Fortunately, a smaller company moved to town and hired a lot of people. Rumor has it that Jake had something to do with bringing the company to town but no one knows for sure. Anyway, people who were still out of work ended up getting together and started taking care of projects around town that needed to be done. We don't like to be idle and the town council was able to get funding from the state for the materials we needed." JoAnne beamed with pride as she spoke. "But please don't misunderstand. We aren't a town of people looking for handouts. We like to take care of ourselves and the state is helping us to do it. The townspeople provide the labor and everyo.ne benefits"

"I'm impressed!" Sue was genuine in her response. From the moment she arrived, she sensed something was different about the town and its residents.

"And I can guarantee you that Earl told someone about the pothole on Route 87 that flattened your tire and it was fixed within a few days."

"This truly is a unique gem of a town," Sue marveled, remembering that Zac had also told her it was a town of hard-working people. Yet they still seemed to have time to enjoy life. She was starting to become envious.

"And wouldn't you know it, not long ago the company that moved their manufacturing to China announced they are going to reopen their plant here. Guess they couldn't get the same quality work over there." JoAnne pointed to a door they were approaching. "Here we are. Best bakery in town!" She held the door open for Sue, who was impressed by the aromas that greeted her as she stepped into the busy shop.

Sue had seen small-town bakeries before but this one might just take the prize! So many delicious treats lined the shelves that she didn't know which looked more enticing. Doughnuts, pastries, cakes, pies, cookies, breads…it was sweet sensory overload. She regretted having such a big breakfast.

"I recommend the banana bread," JoAnne suggested as they perused the pastries. "They have it with walnuts, chocolate chips and plain and they are all delicious. But you order whatever you want. My treat." Before Sue could object, JoAnne put her hand up. "I insist! I appreciate you taking the time to talk with me this morning. I'm hoping to get some travel tips from a pro and that's certainly worth a cup of coffee and a pastry!"

After obtaining their respective sweet delights and freshly brewed coffees, the ladies sat at a table in the window and watched people walking by as they chatted. JoAnne wanted to know how Sue got started writing about traveling, her favorite travel tips, her secrets for finding out-of-the-way gems in each town and so much more. And Sue was happy to regale her with as many stories as she wanted to hear. She had been doing the interviewing and exploring for so long, it was nice to sit and talk about what she had gleaned from all the traveling she had done and perhaps relive some of her favorite moments.

"I'm sorry, you must think I'm a rube." JoAnne paused as she realized she had been peppering Sue with so many questions. "I've been so relentless. You gotta be tired of me by now!"

"Quite the opposite. I rarely get to talk one-on-one like this with someone who is so enthusiastic about travel. But now I want to ask you a question. What is it that makes you want to see the world? A sad statistic is that most people don't have any interest in traveling outside the country where they were born and many people rarely travel more than 100 miles from where they grew up."

"Oh that's easy. I read the article you wrote about visiting Pigeon Forge, Tennessee and Dollywood at Christmas. You said it was straight out of a movie. So many decorations you didn't know where to look first and everywhere you looked was a new, wondrous sight. You described the town and the park with such great detail that I could picture everything. What you wrote about the way the decorations made you feel had a special impact on me. I remember you described a train set you saw that was just like the one your daddy would put under the tree every year when you were little. You wrote about all the wonderful memories it brought back and that the whole experience made you feel like a kid again. As I read it, I told myself that I had to see that place one day." JoAnne slapped Sue's knee as she broke into a broad smile and continued. "And you know what? I did! Went there two years ago!"

"And did it make you feel like a kid again?"

"It did!" JoAnne was grinning from ear to ear. "I absolutely loved it. And I can't wait for my next trip."

"Then my mission to inspire travel has been a success!" Sue was truly pleased to meet someone that had been motivated by her life's work. Reading comments on a webpage from people who read her articles was not at all like talking to someone who had been inspired to travel by her words. *Guess it's worth all the work after all.* "Now the big question is, where do you plan to travel to next."

Without hesitation, JoAnne proclaimed that Greece was next on her list of places to visit. "I know it's quite a jump to go from living here all my life to traveling to Greece. They'll probably look at me funny because of my accent and think I'm crazy because I don't know a lick of Greek. But I saw a movie that was filmed there and it's absolutely beautiful. I want to stay in one of those white houses on the side of a hill overlooking the ocean, relaxing in the sunshine and watching the sunset every night for a week! Might even try a little European-style sunbathing," she finished with a wink.

Sue smiled. "You mid-western rebel!"

JoAnne shrugged with a mischievous smile. "When in Rome…"

"You'll love Greece. It's the most relaxing place I've been in Europe. But let me give you a travel tip. The first non-English speaking country I ever traveled to was Italy. Before I left home, I learned to say 'Excuse me. I don't speak Italian. Do you speak English?' Smartest thing I ever did in preparing for a trip. It made a huge difference in how people reacted to me when I used the phase. You'd be surprised at how much people appreciate you trying to speak to them in their native tongue rather than repeating the same thing over and over slowly and loudly in a language they can't understand no matter how slowly and loudly you speak it! Rookie mistake made by a lot of travelers from the US. It's best to realize that even though English is spoken in a lot of countries as a second language, not everyone you run into in a foreign country knows how to speak it. Learning a phrase or two in Greek will go a long way towards a satisfying travel experience!"

"I never thought about that but it's a great tip. Thanks!" JoAnne made a mental note to follow the sound advice.

Sue dug into her bag for a note pad. "So now that you've picked my brain, how about you let me pick yours?"

JoAnne laughed at the request. "What could I possibly tell you about traveling? You've been everywhere I want to go!"

Sue appreciated her send of humor. "I don't need your advice on traveling. But I'd like to know a townsperson's perspective on Jake and his cowboys."

"Oh that's easy. I can talk about them all day. Well, at least about one of the cowboys." It was fairly obvious she was bursting to tell something personal.

"Fire away. I'm free all afternoon!"

JoAnne settled into her chair. "Well, I don't know if I mentioned it but I'm dating one of the cowboys that works at the ranch. Dusty. Have you met him?"

"As a matter-of-fact, I talked to him yesterday. Unfortunately, he didn't have a whole lot of cowboy holiday traditions to share with me." Sue had actually been a bit put off by Dusty. He seemed aloof and, she thought, not very sharp.

"He's not a real talker and definitely not someone that's too much into the holidays. But he's a really nice guy and we have a lot of fun together."

"Are you two serious?" Sue thought JoAnne could do better.

"We've been dating almost a year but I don't really know." She didn't want to bring up the thing that was holding her back from getting serious about Dusty. He had potential but certainly wasn't living up to it. "We both work crazy hours and don't get as much time to spend with each other as I'd like. Kinda hard to really know someone when you both work a lot."

Sue liked JoAnne and hoped that she figured things out with Dusty before she got her heart broken. "Well then, what can you tell me about Jake. It seems a lot of people think highly of him. I even overheard someone at the diner this morning saying what a great guy he is."

"That's because everyone in town knows it's true. It might seem too good to be real but he is just a wonderful man. He does so much for this town and the people really appreciate him."

Even though Jake wasn't the focus of her article, he owned the ranch that was at the center of it and Sue wanted to know more about him. *For my readers or for myself?* she pondered. "Can you give me some examples?"

JoAnne sat straight up in her chair to emphasize what she was about to say. "I can give you dozens! For example, every year we have a Thanksgiving parade in town. It used to be sponsored by the factory before they moved to China. But every year since the factory has been closed, Jake has donated the money it takes to put on the parade. Every year he buys the little league softball team new uniforms and he just donated money to repair the school playground. When the only fine dining restaurant in town was about to go under after the factory closed, he bought it and helped reorganize the business so they could stay open. I'm telling you, things wouldn't be the same around here without him."

"You make him sound like a saint. Surely he has some faults. He can't be that perfect!" Sue was starting to feel like there was some hero-worshiping going on where the owner of The Big M was concerned.

"Well, good luck finding 'em. The only fault I could ever find in him was his kids. Spoiled, rotten brats, both of 'em!"

Sue was taken aback by the sudden change of attitude. "That's a strong description!"

"It's an accurate description. Jake and Mary used to bring the kids into the diner when they first came to the ranch, before they got things rolling. The daughter's name was Cheryl…can't remember the boy's name. But it was easy to see both of them were spoiled, simple as that. The food was never good enough for them. The fries weren't crispy enough, the burger bun wasn't brioche, we didn't have some special sauce they wanted, blah, blah, blah. And they had no problem with being vocal about what they didn't like. Eventually Jake just stopped bringing them in. Guess he didn't want them embarrassing him anymore." JoAnne shook her head in disgust. "My brother and I acted up once when our mama took us out and she said if we ever did something like that again, we'd never see the outside world again until we were 21!" She laughed at the memory. "And it worked! We were the best behaved kids you'd ever want to see. Guess Jake never had that talk with his kids."

Sue was perplexed. Jake didn't seem the type to have spoiled kids. *Maybe that's the reason he doesn't like talking about them* she pondered. "He's only briefly mentioned his children. Doesn't seem like they're close."

"That's putting it mildly." JoAnne chortled. "Those brats went off to college and I never heard of them coming back. Even when their mother was dying, I heard they came to the ranch and left pretty quickly. I think there is a lot of bad feelings between them and their father. Don't know that they have ever been back since Mary passed."

"That's very unfortunate." All Sue could think about was how she'd give anything to spend even an hour with her parents again. Jake's kids at least had one of their parents alive and well but it appeared they didn't seem interested in a relationship with him. *What a pity* she thought. *What could have happened that was so bad these kids don't talk to their father? Some people don't know how to appreciate the gifts they have right in front of them.* Wanting to move back to the subject of the ranch, she tried to be tactful. "Did you go to Thanksgiving dinner at the ranch this year?"

Without realizing it, JoAnne had gotten herself worked up talking about Jake's kids so the question offered a welcome respite from the thoughts swirling in her head. "Absolutely! I wouldn't have missed it. There was so much delicious food! We did our best to eat it all but it seemed to keep multiplying!" Pleased to move onto a happier subject, she continued. "When we got back to my place, Dusty and I just passed out in bed. So much food!"

"I hear a lot of the people who vacation at the ranch come back for Thanksgiving every year."

JoAnne nodded. "It's really quite a special event."

Sue scribbled some notes, then continued to ask about the ranch, the cowboys, the cowboy-themed vacations people came to enjoy, anything she could think of to ask about so she could get a local's perspective on the ranch and the people involved. JoAnne seemed to love talking about everything as much as Sue like hearing about it.

After an hour or so, Sue had more notes than she could use and decided it was time to start working them into the story. During a pause in the conversation, she dug into her bag and retrieved a business card. "Thanks very much for providing me so much information on the ranch and the town. It's really going to give some great context to my piece." She handed the card to JoAnne. "Please give me a call when you get back from Greece. I want to hear all about your trip."

Joanne suddenly turned into a giddy schoolgirl. "Oh, you don't want to hear from me and what I think about a place where you've already been."

"I absolutely do want to hear about your trip! If you don't call me, I'll be very disappointed!"

The look on her face told JoAnne she was sincere. "OK, I'll give you a call. Should be around next August if everything goes as planned. It'll take me that long to learn some phrases in Greek!"

She thought Sue's suggestion was excellent advice. "Can you imagine me talking Greek with this accent?!?"

"You'll do just fine. And I hate to cut this short but I need to get back to work. I'm supposed to be at the ranch early tomorrow so I need to get some writing done today." They rose from the table and hugged, preparing to leave. But Sue wasn't sure why she hugged JoAnne. She generally wasn't a 'hugger'. In her business, meeting so many people, she was a believer in the handshake as being a proper salutation. She hugged her close friends, not people she had only known for a few days.

Walking back to the inn, Sue tried to figure out what was so different about this project. She'd literally been to hundreds of similar towns and had never hugged a person she met in any of them even though she still kept in touch with some of the people she'd met in her travels. But ever since she had been in the unusually charming town of Spruce, getting to know the hard working people who made up the population and spending time on Jake's ranch riding horses and hunting for trees, she felt different.... relaxed....better.

*****

Wayne walked up to the main house as Jake was coming through the door. He hated making the walk but he knew he had no choice. Safety for all concerned was paramount on a working ranch. "Mornin' boss."

"Mornin' Wayne. Everything good this morning?"

"We've got a problem."

Jake knew that Wayne was someone who took care of problems himself and rarely brought them to him so he had a good idea of what this was about. "Who is it?"

"Dusty."

"Have you tested him?"

"Don't need to. He's got the three S's: stumblin', slurrin' and stupid."

Jake was disappointed. He had high hopes for Dusty since he reminded him a little of his own son. But, unfortunately, he wasn't surprised after the encounter they had following Sue's first visit. "OK, guess we got no choice."

Wayne nodded. "I'll take care of it."

But Jake thought this might be an opportunity to hopefully provide direction to someone who desperately needed it, whether he knew it or not. "No, send him up. I'll do it." He turned and went back into the house to wait. *I hate this shit.*

About five minutes later, Dusty walked in to find Jake in his office at the front of the house. "What's up boss?"

Jake was seated at his desk, feeling it was best to keep things formal even if the conversation might eventually take a more personal turn. He motioned to the chair positioned across from the desk. "Have a seat."

He was feeling a bit aloof. "Uh oh. Guess I'm in trouble." The serious expression on Jake's face quickly told Dusty this was no time for joking.

"You could say that. You know why?"

Dusty tried to straighten up as he sat down. "Not sure boss."

"You're high."

Dusty's laugh was half-hearted if Jake had ever heard one. He avoided eye contact as he choked out a response. "No I'm not boss, really."

To Jake, it was disappointing that Dusty wasn't man enough to admit he was caught. *Just like a kid with his hand in the cookie jar.* "Don't bother. What you do on your own time is your concern. But when you show up like this to work, you put others in danger, not to mention yourself and the herd. Can't have it. Won't have it."

"C'mon boss. I just had a longer weekend than usual but I'm good."

"No, you're not. And you've been warned not to bring your party life to the ranch. Yet here you are. So you know where we're at."

Dusty was desperate to find a way out of the situation he knew was brewing. "C'mon Jake, lighten up. I don't do anything that's not pretty well accepted and even legal in a lot of places."

Jake was started to get tired of Dusty's cavalier attitude. "You and I both know we aren't talking about a joint you smoked. You're on something much harder." Jake knew at one point in his life, he could have been on Dusty's side of this conversation. Which was one of the many reasons he bought the ranch. In his former life, substance abuse was rampant and after a taste, he knew he wanted no part of it for himself or his kids, who could have easily been sucked in. "Crap like that puts my people, my herd and my ranch in danger and I won't stand for it."

"Seems like a bit of an overstatement to me."

Jake felt himself ready to explode. But instead he paused, took a breath and considered his next words carefully. "And that is a typical statement from someone who refuses to see anyone's point-of-view that doesn't agree with theirs. Have you ever wondered why there aren't more young cowboys and cowgirls on this ranch?"

"Not really. Just figured you didn't like young people."

"I have nothing against young people. What I don't like are people who refuse to accept that there are rules to be followed. And consequences when those rules are broken. I find that a disproportionate number of people who think they don't have to follow the rules are young and typically don't think about what happens when laws and rules are broken."

"Maybe the rules need to change. Or maybe there just shouldn't be so many rules to begin with."

"Spoken like a true…" Jake stopped himself before he said something he might regret. He stared at Dusty for several moments. And to his credit, Dusty didn't say anything further, perhaps sensing that he had reached the point of Jake's tolerance in their conversation. "Rules are in place for a reason. If those rules have outlived their usefulness and need to be changed, then work to convince others of why the change is needed. But it's not enough to simply say rules need to be changed because you don't agree with them. And until they are changed, you don't get to arbitrarily decide which rules you don't have to follow. When you are in charge, when you are the owner or when you are the boss, you can make the rules. But until then, you need to respect those in charge and follow the rules or deal with the ramifications of your choices."

The adrenaline rushing through his veins quickly had a sobering effect on Dusty as the gravity of his situation started to sink in. "Are you sure there's no way around it?"

"You know there isn't. You need to pack your stuff and get off the ranch. You've got an hour."

"Please boss. Isn't there any way I can change your mind?"

Jake stared into his eyes as he tried to formulate the right words to make the person he felt had great potential sitting across from him realize he needed to make a change in his life before it was too late. "The only thing you have the power to change is yourself. You have a drug problem. Get it straightened out and we can talk about your future. But you can't do anything at the moment other than pack."

Dusty started to panic. He couldn't lose his job. He loved working on the ranch. What else would he do? And what would JoAnne say. She had warned him this could happen. But he ignored her warning and now it was actually happening! "Boss, I swear, I don't have a drug problem."

"Pretty sure you do."

"No, I don't." Dusty grew adamant in his assertion, even though he clearly had no reason to be.

Jake had seen this so many times before and hated seeing yet another person in denial. In the past, he'd had friends, co-workers and employees who all thought they had their recreational drug use under control. But no one ever did and eventually, it caught up to them and their lives fell apart. Maybe this time he could help someone before it was too late. "Let me ask you this. You no longer have a job. I assume that's a problem for you."

Dusty held his head low. "Damn right it is."

"And you lost your job because of drugs, right?"

"That's what you're sayin'."

"You know damn well that's the reason!" Jake wanted Dusty to admit this one simple fact or there was nothing he could do to help.

Eventually Dusty replied in a hushed voice. "Yeah, I know."

"So if you lost your job because of drugs, and it's a problem for you to lose your job, then you have a drug problem! Don't be so cocky that you can't admit your weakness. You're giving into something that will ruin your future, you're entire life, unless you do something about it. Now! I've warned you in the past but now you're at the point where you have to make a decision about your future. Are you gonna waste it or are you gonna be a responsible individual and take care of your personal business before you become a burden to your family and possibly make a mistake that you can't fix? Or worse, cause someone else harm. Right now you're on the path for a wasted life. You don't see it because you think you can handle anything. I've seen people who thought they had it all under control and could stop any time and all that crap. But they didn't and they couldn't and lots of them ended up in sad circumstances in the end with no family, no friends, no money. Don't be one of those people, don't be a statistic. Show how strong you actually are and take care of your problem. Only you can make the decision and do the work to get yourself back on track. You're a good man. I can see that. You just need to prove it. To yourself."

Dusty was defeated. He looked at Jake for a brief moment. Maybe his now former boss was right. But at that moment, all he wanted to do was get out of there, pack his meager belongings and get off the ranch. He wanted to hide himself away. From Jake; from JoAnne; from the world. His head was swimming as he slowly got up. He felt lost. He tried to speak but couldn't think of anything worthwhile to say. He just wanted to get out of that room, to run out of that room as fast and as far away as he could. He would handle whatever needed handling tomorrow. Today, he just wanted to run. But somehow, in his foggy head he realized that running wasn't the solution. Without another word, he turned and walked out.

CHAPTER 10

The Big M ranch was buzzing with activity when Sue arrived, hoping to conduct a few more interviews so she could finish her article early. Wayne was barking out orders as Jake came down from the house with Bernie leading the way. Upon seeing Sue, Bernie ran to her as fast as he could, ready to feel her long fingernails scratching behind his ears. As Jake met up with them, he marveled, "I still can't get over how he has taken to you. He usually warms up to people at a snail's pace."

Sue squatted down to scratch Bernie's neck. "It's simple. We understand each other!" She kissed Bernie on the forehead as she held his head between her hands, then stood up. "Looks like everyone's getting ready to do some work."

"Oh, this isn't work for them. This is what they were born to do!"

Wayne approached Sue from behind. "Mornin' ma'am."

She wheeled around revealing a broad smile while slapping him on the shoulder. "Would you please stop with that 'ma'am' crap?! You make me feel old!"

He tipped his hat and matched her smile. "Sorry ma'am, just doin' like my mama taught me." He winked as he turned to Jake. "Everyone's ready to go. Any last thoughts?"

"Just don't stay any longer than 4-5 days. I want everyone to be back in plenty of time for Christmas."

"You got it boss."

As Wayne turned towards the anxiously waiting group of cowpokes, Dolly came rushing from the house with a basket. "Hold on," she shouted as she ran towards them. "These just cooled off enough for me to pack them."

Wayne's face lit up with excitement. "Are these your famous oatmeal chocolate chip cookies?" Sue could almost see his mouth watering.

"Indeed they are. First batch of many I'll be making for the party. And the lot of you get the first taste. Just don't eat them all at once," Dolly cautioned. "They need to hold you until you get back."

"I'll dole them out sparingly." He gave her a peck on the cheek. "What did we do to deserve you?"

She blushed as Sue wondered if there wasn't something more than just mutual admiration between the two. "I'll never know but you better keep it up. You wouldn't know what to do if I wasn't around." Dolly stared at him for just a second longer than anyone without a romantic notion would.

"That's a fact!" Wayne took the basket and with a wink and smile, headed down the hill. With the basket of treasured treats tucked safely inside the wagon, he mounted Lucy and gave the signal to move out. Like a well-rehearsed group of dancers, the cowboys and cowgirls moved out to the pasture and started herding the cattle, pointing them towards the southern part of the ranch.

Sue watched the activity with appreciation and disappointment. "Where are they going?"

"To the southern pasture for a few days. With the mild fall, there is still plenty of fresh grass down there for them to feed on so it makes sense to let them do it while they can. Once the snow comes, they only have winter wheat to feed on until spring."

"Is the fresh grass that much better for them?"

"Absolutely. Makes a big difference in their size and overall health. And the healthier the cow, the better the meat!"

Sue nodded. "Makes sense. The beef here is the best I've ever eaten. Is it true that Montana has some of the best grazing grass in the entire country?"

"Someone did their research!" Jake smiled with appreciation. "It's true, so I'd like for them to feed on as much of it as they can. Gotta take advantage of these weather patterns before the snow flies."

"Glad it's working out for you but I had been hoping to talk to a few more cowboys today. I didn't know you were planning to move the herd." Sue became anxious. "Everyone on the drive will miss the festival!"

"And most of them are glad of it!" Jake chuckled. "Remember that I told you cowboys don't typically go for the traditional Christmas parties and stuff like that. The festival falls under the heading of Christmas traditions cowboys don't really care about. The drive is a good excuse for them to not attend. The only thing that might have enticed them into going this year is the entertainment. I heard a rumor that Skip Ewing is doing a surprise performance."

"I'm not familiar with him. Who is he?"

Jake was genuinely surprised. "With as much as you know about Christmas music, I'm surprised. Skip is an amazing songwriter and his Christmas stuff is great. Have you never heard 'It Wasn't His Child'?"

"I've heard it by Trisha Yearwood. It's a great song."

"Skip wrote it and recorded it before anyone else. A lot of people have covered it but Skip's original version is the best."

"I'll have to listen to it. I wonder how they got him to perform."

"He lives on a ranch in Wyoming and has an affinity for this lifestyle and the type of people who live here. His success allows him to enjoy life as he wishes and he probably wants to give back. He's a good guy."

"You sound like an expert on him."

Jake became aware he might be revealing too much. "Not an expert. Just a fan." Before the 'investigative reporter' in Sue could come out, he changed the subject. "I'm going into town to take care of a few details regarding the festival. If you want to tag along, I've thought of a few things that might work for your article. Give me a few minutes and we can get going." He quickly walked towards the house.

Bernie was torn between following him and being with Sue. But as soon as she started towards the house, he went running up the hill with his tail wagging.

The festival was quickly becoming an event she was looking forward to attending as much as she was looking forward to learning more about Jake. She was certain she had just begun to scratch the surface of his story.

*****

The ride into town had proved fruitful for Sue as Jake provided a few things that would work nicely in her article. It was starting to look like she would be able to turn in a quality piece after all!

As Jake met with Mayor Taylor to make sure everything was in place for a smooth festival the next evening, Sue didn't want to impose herself on the conversation and stood a few feet away as they conversed. Watching the preparations happening in the town square, she could hear most of their conversation and it occurred to her that Jake took an unusually strong interest in making sure everything was right for the musical performance.

When the meeting wrapped up, Jake walked over and joined her in watching the activity in the square. "Everything good?" she inquired.

"Looks like it. Skip will go on at 7:00 pm and after his set, he and the mayor will light the tree. Tickets were already selling well but with news of the surprise musical guest getting out, the festival will probably sell out. Looks like it'll be another successful year."

"I couldn't help but hear Taylor saying you might have had something to do with getting Skip to appear." Sue adopted a mock investigative reporter stance as she held an invisible microphone to Jake's mouth. "Care to elaborate?"

He quickly adopted the expression of a celebrity caught in an uncompromising situation. "No comment." There were certain aspects of his life and business that he wasn't ready to share with Sue...or anybody for that matter. But he was starting to wonder if he might change his long-standing stance where she was concerned. Maybe he was finally ready to come out from behind the wall where he had been hiding for so long. But it wasn't going to happen at that moment so he smiled and changed the subject. "Are you hungry?"

"Famished!" She was certain there was much more to Jake than met the eye but her instincts told her it was not the time to press for details he wasn't prepared to share. So, eating seemed like a good idea since she had skipped breakfast. Discovering Jake's story could wait a while longer.

CHAPTER 11

Sue awakened quite content. The town's Christmas festival seemed to go off without a hitch and Skip Ewing's performance was exceptional, after a slight technical problem with the sound was fixed. He entertained his attentive audience with stories and music that spoke directly to the people of Spruce and their way of life. It was obvious to her that Jake's assessment of Skip and his appreciation of life on a ranch was accurate. Everyone seemed to have a great time and even though Jake tried to be inconspicuous, anyone who saw him went out of their way to express their appreciation, knowing the festival wouldn't have happened without his support. As he walked her back to the inn, there was a bite in the air that made Sue want to snuggle up to him to keep warm. But she caught herself before grabbing his arm to wrap it around her. *Where did that urge come from??*

Back in her room after she had breakfast, Sue's mood turned dark. She now had no real reason to stay any longer. Her research was basically done and she only stayed the extra couple days because she wanted to take part in the festival. She had met so many wonderful people during her time in town and they had all asked if she was staying for the festival. And while she was glad she did, Christmas was less than a week away and she needed to get home. She could finish the article in her apartment. But she knew in her heart she would rather finish it in Spruce!

Reminiscing on all the excitement of the last couple weeks, Sue realized she had barely spoken to Melanie or Jackie. Wayne was right! Like the vacationers at the ranch, she didn't miss her phone ringing constantly at all! But she did miss her friends and figured she should let them know she was alive and well and headed home. She picked up the phone next to her bed and dialed Jackie's number, hoping she would answer a number she didn't recognize. After a few rings, her voice came on the line. "Hello?"

"Hey there. It's Sue!"

Jackie couldn't hide her surprise. "Hey there yourself, stranger. Where are you? This isn't your phone number."

"I'm calling from the inn."

"Everything OK?" Concern was evident in her tone.

Sue laughed but realized her friends were probably worried about her. "I'm fine. And I'm sorry I haven't been in touch. But I've been busy with my research but at the same time having the most fun I've ever had preparing an article!"

"So, that's it. Just as I predicted, you've found a hot cowboy and forgot about the two of us."

"Well, I have to say, I think I have fallen in love while I've been here." She couldn't resist playing with her friend, knowing her sense of humor.

"I knew I was right! What's his name?"

"Lucy. She's a beauty!" She could almost hear Jackie's brain trying to formulate the correct response. "She's tall, has a great rear section and a beautiful, long snout with ears that twitch when I talk to her while feeding her apples."

After a pregnant pause, Jackie finally choked out a response. "I'm really hoping we aren't discussing a human."

Sue burst out laughing as she explained Lucy was the horse she rode while on the Christmas Tree Hunt. "I have so much more to tell you but for now I just wanted to let you know that I'm leaving today. I'll call you when I get home."

"You better. We need to finalize our Christmas Eve Brunch plans!"

"I know. And I want to tell you about everything I've seen and done here. It's such a wonderful place!"

Jackie felt there was something odd about her friend. "You sure you're OK? You sound different."

She wasn't sure how to respond. Of course she was fine but she did feel different. She also knew she didn't want to discuss what was going on with her at that moment. "I'm just nice and relaxed. And I need to get going. I'll talk to you soon." As she hung up the phone, she wondered if there was more truth to her statement about falling in love while in Spruce than she realized.

*****

Having said goodbye to Zac, Earl and JoAnne on her way out of town, Sue pulled into the Big M one last time. She spotted Jake standing on the front porch as she drove up and parked. He was fixated on the darkening skies to the north and as she got out of her car, she noticed the breeze had started to pick up and the first snowflakes of the season began to fall. Jake was so immersed in watching the gathering clouds and trying to raise someone on the radio that he didn't notice her as she approached the porch. "Hey Cowboy."

Jake glanced briefly towards her. "Sorry, didn't see you," was all he said as he continued alternately looking at the foreboding northern sky and the two-way radio in his hand, concern clearly shown on his face .

"Everything OK?"

"Just got an updated weather report. There's a blizzard forming in Canada and it's expected to drop down this way fast. If it's as bad as they are forecasting, it could strand the herd."

"Can't Wayne just bring them back?"

"Where they're at, I can't reach them on the radio to warn him. The hills and valleys wreak havoc with the radio signals. And, as you know, cell signals are no better."

Sue could see the concern consuming Jake, which she was starting to share. "Can't they ride out the storm?"

"Cattle have a natural instinct about snow and will lay down when it starts to fall so they can keep the ground beneath them dry. Allows them to stay warm until the storm passes."

"So cattle were surviving blizzards long before we came along. Seems like they know what they're doing and should be OK, right?"

"They would be as long as they had food. But the pasture they are in is in a valley with only one way in and out. That pass gets blocked quickly by these kinds of storms. Then, when the sun comes out, the snow buildup in the pass melts just enough to become a solid block of ice when it refreezes at night. It completely cuts off access to the pasture until the spring thaw. If they get stuck in there, they'll starve."

Dolly came rushing from the house. "Jake, another weather update is now calling for 18 to 24 inches of snowfall in the next 24 hours."

"Damn! I never should've sent the herd out there." He started to pace the porch.

Sue suddenly appreciated the gravity of the situation as she looked at Dolly, who would have none of Jake second-guessing himself. "There was no prediction of this storm and you know it. The weather hasn't changed this drastically so quickly in years but it's happening now. So what do you want to do?"

Jake took one more look at the sky, then at his empty pasture, then at Sue and finally at Dolly. "Brew thermoses of coffee and pack some jerky. I've gotta go get them."

Dolly didn't need to be told twice. She was gone in a flash and in the kitchen preparing the essentials she knew Jake and the cowboys would need.

Jake looked at Sue, suddenly realizing he hadn't been expecting her, yet there she was. "Sorry, I gotta get ready to go. Walk with me if you need something." He started down to the barn with her and Bernie on his heels.

"I just came to say goodbye and thank you for everything." Jake stopped short and turned to face her. "You're leaving? You're finished with the article?" Before she could answer, he turned and started towards the barn again.

"Yes...and no. I'm leaving because I have a deadline to hit but I'm not finished with the story yet. Figured I'd get it done at home. You and your cowboys gave me lots of great info. I just have to put it all together and there are too many distractions here for me to finish it in time." As they approached the barn, she finally noticed that there was no one else around. "Where is everyone?"

"Dusty's gone. Stacey has a few days off and Cowboy Bill, James and the others are with part of the herd up north. It'll take them too long to get back here and help."

"Are you going out there by yourself?!?"

"Can't wait. And I won't be alone. Bernie will be with me."

Bernie appeared to be looking forward to whatever was coming his way while Jake calmly but anxiously saddled his horse. He was obviously more worried about his people and the herd than himself. "OK, but....if I can be of any help, I'm willing to come with you." Even as the words left her mouth, she thought she sounded foolish and fully expected Jake to laugh at the prospect.

He looked at her for several moments with a stare that clearly showed he thought her offer was anything but foolish. "Not in those clothes. Got anything warm with you?"

"If you really think I can help instead of being in the way, I have warm clothes in the car." She so hoped he was serious.

"With your riding skills, no way I'm going to turn down your offer. Get changed and I'll saddle up a horse for you." He was thankful to have another rider for this. It wasn't going to be an easy move if he didn't get there before the snow really began to fly!

Sue started running to her car before he changed his mind.

*****

It wasn't long after the decision was made to ride out that the horses were saddled and loaded up with the necessities. Dolly looked confident she would see them all soon as Jake, Sue and Bernie set out on their mission. The wind had started to pick up and snow was falling more steadily. Jake pointed out to Sue that it wasn't lying on the ground yet. "It's been warm enough that the ground isn't frozen. But that'll change soon. It's already below freezing and it's supposed to drop one degree every hour through the rest of the day." He picked up the pace to a brisk trot and Sue had no trouble keeping up. While their mission was serious, she was thrilled to be riding again. And the weather, while causing a serious issue for the herd, just made her feel more like Christmas was coming. She couldn't have been more content.

In less than an hour, they spotted the herd in the distance. The snow had become heavy and steady and was starting to cover the ground. The cattle were following their instincts as Jake went into a full gallop in order to get to Wayne quickly as Sue held back a bit so Bernie could easily keep up.

The serious expression on the face of his boss as he approached told Wayne all he needed to know. "Seeing you tells me this is more than just a snow squall."

Jake nodded with a somber expression. "A Canadian blizzard has formed and it'll be here soon. Couldn't raise you on the radio so we came to help you get the herd back. We have coffee and biscuits if anyone needs to fuel up while you get organized."

Wayne nodded towards Sue and Bernie as they approached. "We'll need all the help we can muster. And if this storm turns into the monster it's looking like it might, we better stop wagging our tongues and get going." He turned his mount towards the wranglers and started barking orders to get the herd ready to move back to the main pasture. "And don't let them lay down. If they start getting settled, we'll never get them moving!"

Once his cowboys were set, he went back to Jake and Sue, giving them instructions on what he needed from them. "Just make sure that anything trying to stray from the herd doesn't get too far." Jake glanced at Sue, expecting to see a look of panic at the prospect of having to get a stray back to the herd. But her expression made it clear that she was looking forward to the challenge and was confident in her abilities, even though he was certain she hadn't worked with live cattle since she won her Little Britches trophy! Bernie was ready too and went into action as soon as he heard the order to move the herd.

With the snow coming down harder than ever, the drive to the other side of the pass started. Several cattle tried to lie down but someone was on each one of them before they could get settled. Eventually, the herd was moving steadily through the storm, which had now completely darkened the skies. The fierce wind was blowing the snow horizontally as they proceeded slowly towards their destination. Sue pulled her collar tight around her neck, thankful she had packed the thick, warm coat that now helped ward off the storm.

As the herd moved slowly, in the distance Sue saw a few of the cattle trying to veer off. She watched as the experienced cowpokes expertly brought the strays back to the herd. While she would have liked to be part of what she had just watched, she realized that it was much smarter to leave the real cattle herding to the experts, certain the old saying 'it's just like riding a bike, you never forget how' probably didn't apply in her case. Bringing up the rear of the herd with Jake made the most sense, knowing that cattle like to follow each other and it was very unlikely the animals towards the rear would do anything but follow the animal in front of them, especially in such a storm.

Even with the snow and the wind and the cold, Sue was elated. She felt more alive than she had in quite some time. The feeling she experienced riding a horse was like nothing else and she had forgotten how happy it made her. She always felt she made the correct career choice but being at The Big M had stirred up doubts she had suppressed long ago, she had thought, for good. She never liked questioning her choices. *Don't start now!* But she had felt different since arriving in Spruce and spending time on the ranch. Even Jackie heard something in her voice that morning. Thoughts of doubt and confusion were swirling in her head as violently as the snow blowing around it.

As she struggled with the thoughts invading her mind, Sue was brought back to her current situation by the sight of two cattle trying to stray and head for the shelter of nearby trees. Jake started towards them with Bernie following. Suddenly, the strays split up! One was headed towards the trees but the other was trying to double-back, seemingly confused by the storm. Jake took off after the one going for the trees while Sue went after the one headed back to where they had just come from. With instincts she didn't know she still had, she weaved back and forth in front of the animal to stop it from progressing any further away. Jake quickly had his cow back in line with the rest of the herd then instinctively started towards Sue and her stray. He didn't go far before stopping and watching with admiration as she and Bernie worked in tandem to thwart the animal's plan and expertly brought it back to the herd in the blowing snow. To Jake, Sue continued to be full of surprises. Surprises he appreciated.

They moved slowly through the pasture as the storm intensified. Eventually, Sue thought she could make out what might be the passage Jake was worried about. Once through the area, he gave her a thumbs-up sign. "That's what I was worried about!" he shouted over the wind. It was a relief to her that they had at least made it through the worst section and that the most worrisome part of the journey was behind them. But they still had a long way to go before the cattle were where they needed to be.

*****

The sun was just starting to touch the horizon as the herd began to move into the main pasture. Not that anyone could see it! The snow was coming down harder than ever and clouds had obscured the sun hours ago. As the herd moved through the pasture gate, two of the cowboys counted each head as the rest of them continued to push until the last head was through. As Wayne closed the gate, he called to one of his counters. "How many?"

"352."

The other counter nodded.

With their mission complete, everyone was quick to head to the stable and unsaddle their horses, get them dried off and covered with blankets before heading for the warmth of their bunkhouses. Stacey, having come back to the ranch early once she saw the storm gathering, greeted Jake and Sue, volunteering to take care of their horses so they could get inside.

Wayne approached Jake and Sue with a relieved smile. "Didn't lose a single head! Thanks for your help."

Sue couldn't contain her exhilaration. "That was awesome!"

Jake beamed with appreciation. "Glad you had fun. But it was a seriously challenging drive. *You* were what was awesome!"

Wayne gave her an appreciative smile. "You should be proud of yourself. You ever get tired of working in the city, I've got a job for you right here!"

She blushed. Every skill she had ever learned had come flooding back to her that afternoon. She felt so comfortable in the saddle that the reality of the fact she hadn't done anything like that in years never entered her mind. Maybe she had been wrong when she doubted herself all those years ago.

Jake turned towards Wayne. "Go get warmed up. I'm sure Dolly has a big pot of chili waiting for everyone." Then he gave a wink. "I'll send a couple bottles down to help take off the chill. Have a good evening."

CHAPTER 12

As much as she enjoyed the drive, Sue was happy to be inside the warm house and out of the storm, which was intensifying rapidly. Dolly was in the bunkhouse making sure everyone had hot food but left a note which Sue pointed out to Jake. 'Latest forecast is 24 to 30 inches. Not supposed to let up until late morning.' "So much for the mild fall," she stated matter-of-factly as she sat down and struggled to remove her boots.

Jake bent down to help her, knowing she wasn't considering the impact the storm would have on her plans. "I hate to be the bearer of bad news but this storm means more than just an end to the mild weather. You're likely stuck here for a few days."

"A few days?!?"

"At least. Once the storm ends sometime tomorrow, we need to clear the road to the highway, and it'll be at least a day before the highway itself is cleared all the way to the airport, which will probably be shut down for most of tomorrow anyway."

This was news she did not want to hear. "But I need to get back and finish my story!"

"I thought you were leaving because you were done?"

"The first draft is done but I still have to polish it up and submit it to my editor sometime tomorrow."

"No need to panic. You can finish it here."

"But I can't submit it without internet access!" Sue's panic was starting to get the better of her.

He couldn't help but smile. Her perception that missing her deadline was the worst possible thing that could happen reminded him of a time when he used to deal with similar situations and perceptions on a regular basis. But they really meant nothing in the grand scheme of things. It was a time he was thankful to have left in his forgotten past. He had learned long ago that living in a remote location had some drawbacks that simply had to be taken in stride. But the advantages of country living far outweighed whatever complications crept up. "You know, we're pretty modern around here. We have internet and everything." He hoped humor might help to calm her fears. "Once I turn on the box with all the lights and find the password, you can send your article off in one of those e-mail things you think I don't know about." Unfortunately, he didn't sense it was working. At all.

"But I have a million things to do before Christmas! I've spent more time than I planned out here and I have shopping to do and decorations to put up and baking and...I can't be stuck out here for days!"

"Slow down Cowgirl! Tell you what. Why don't you forget about all that stuff and spend Christmas here? The rooms are already prepared for the guests that'll be arriving in a few days and I'm thinking this storm is going to cause a few cancellations." He paused as even he was caught off-guard by his sudden realization that he wanted Sue to stay so they could celebrate the holiday together. But before he could over-examine what he was doing, he continued to try and convince her. "If you spend Christmas here, there's no need to shop and do all the stuff you *have* to do! And you can help prepare for the party. I know Dolly would appreciate it and you'll get to actually experience a 'Cowboy Christmas' at the Big M!"

Sue was exasperated. She sat with one boot still on and leaned her head against the wall behind her as she listened to the hollowing wind. Slowly she started to realize she was panicking over nothing. All she needed was Jake's internet to complete the job she came to do. And if she was being honest with herself, a Christmas at the ranch sounded enticing. Very enticing. She just had to figure out a way to break the news to Melanie and Jackie that, for the first time, she wouldn't be able to make their annual brunch. But that certainly wasn't an insurmountable issue. "It's looking like I might not have much of a choice. But I don't know that I can make any decisions until I warm up! I'm chilled to the bone. And I'm starving!"

"Tell you what. A hot shower will take care of one of your issues. Meet me in the dining room in an hour and I'll make sure the other one is handled as well."

"It's a date!" *Damn!* Sue thought as soon as the words left her lips. *Why did I say that?* She was afraid to look at Jake for fear he would read more into her short statement if he thought she was looking for his reaction. She quickly pulled off her other boot and situated her wet clothing so it would dry while sneaking quick glances at Jake, who seemed to not have a reaction to the three words that had just carelessly blasted from her mouth. Without another word, she picked up her suitcase and made her way upstairs.

*****

Once away from Jake and the words that were lingering in the air, Sue felt more at ease. The thought of a hot shower and dry clothing had never sounded so good. With all the guest rooms ready for the Christmas revelers to arrive, she felt bad for messing one up, knowing Dolly would have to redo it, so she tried not to overtake the entire space. With shampoo in hand, she made her way into the bathroom and turned the shower on as warm as she could stand it. The water felt invigorating and she just stood under the rainfall shower for several minutes, not doing anything but enjoying the heat as it penetrated her body. As she warmed, she reflected on the day's events. *When was the last time I felt so alive, so useful, so unstressed in a stressful situation?* She couldn't answer her own questions. She had felt so good during the cattle drive, so needed, so....successful. *Why?* Was it because Jake needed help and she was there to provide it? Was it because it was imperative they get the herd back to safety? Or was it simply the contentment she felt being on the ranch, around animals and in the company of genuinely good people, one in particular?

Realizing she had been standing in the shower long enough that her fingers were starting to prune, she washed quickly and wrapped herself in the soft towel hanging on the shower door. She was impressed with its quality. Jake obviously didn't spare any detail when it came to the comfort of his guests. It was probably a detail Mary insisted on but Sue was happy to see it didn't change after she passed. While she was certain real cowboys didn't worry about Egyptian cotton towels, she was also certain that people wanting a 'cowboy-experience' vacation didn't necessarily want to leave *all* the niceties of home behind!

After drying her hair as much as she could, she pulled clean jeans and a flannel shirt from her suitcase and dressed. As she combed her still damp hair, she realized her makeup was in a bag still in her car. She wasn't so vain as to even entertain for a moment the thought of making a trek to the car to retrieve it. She didn't wear that much anyway so she didn't think Jake would be too scared seeing her without. Besides, the odors wafting from the kitchen informed her that Dolly was cooking up a delicious meal and her grumbling stomach quickly overrode her vanity.

As Sue made her way to the dining room, she could hear the blizzard winds howling and it made her shiver, even though she was warm and safe. Bernie greeted her as she entered the room where the long table reminded her of movies where wealthy people sit at each end and can barely hear each other as they try to converse. Thankfully she saw that there were two place settings at one corner of the table. *No shouting to each other necessary!* Appropriately, *Let It Snow!* by Andy Williams was playing softly.

She was certain the sound of her stomach was worse than the storm as Jake entered with two plates of steaming food. "Perfect timing!" he beamed, placing the plates on the table. "Dinner is served!" He pulled out the chair for Sue and as she settled in, he poured wine for both of them, then settled into his own chair. He held up his glass and declared, "Bon Appetite!"

Sue sipped the crisp, clean red wine and felt it banish the last bit of cold she felt deep within as it slid down her throat. Then she carefully examined the plate of food before her. "This looks delicious! Dolly outdid herself."

"I beg your pardon!" Jake feigned indignation. "I am the creator of this evening's feast, thank you very much." The mischievous smile on his face told her he was not to be believed.

Sue laughed. "You don't really expect me to believe you created this sumptuous looking meal, do you?"

"Indeed I do. How could you not believe this honest face?!"

His response made her really start to wonder. "OK, I'll bite. Please tell me on what we are about to dine."

Jake was clearly enjoying himself as he described the meal before her. "For a starter, we have fresh mozzarella over sliced tomatoes, sprinkled with basil and dressed with a robust extra virgin olive oil and balsamic vinegar. Then there is asparagus cooked exactly 3 minutes, firm but tender, sprayed with more olive oil, dusted with fresh cracked pepper and shaved parmesan cheese. And for the main dish, chicken breast stuffed with sundried tomatoes, gorgonzola cheese, fresh spinach and coated with my homemade Dijon mustard sauce." He looked at her with a matter-of-fact satisfied smile.

She stared at him for a few moments, dumbfounded. When she found her voice, her statement was simple. "OK, you must have made this meal because someone who doesn't know their way around the kitchen wouldn't even be able to list those ingredients, much less tell me how to put them together."

"Well, it's been a while since I cooked like this...but it seems like an appropriate occasion."

Sue took a bite of the tomatoes and mozzarella and was impressed. Then she took a bite of the chicken and her eyes grew wide with every chew as the tender meat and delicious combination of flavors danced over her taste buds. She really couldn't believe the delicious spread before her was created by the cowboy sitting across from her but she decided to play along a little longer. "Did you used to cook like this often?"

Jake took a big bite of chicken as he was suddenly uncomfortable and wanted time to think. It had been a while since he cooked one of his specialties and he had done so tonight without thinking of the potential consequences, of the questions and discussion that would inevitably follow. But lately he had started to think those consequences were all in his head. Maybe he subconsciously made one of his signature dishes so he could talk to Sue about more than the ranch and what cowboys do at Christmas. She was different than the other women he had met in the years since Mary had passed. *Am I finally ready?* He swallowed, took a deep breath and replied. "I have a confession." He paused again. "Tonight you are dining with Chef J." He braced himself for what he was certain would be the thousand questions headed his way.

Sue laughed and didn't even look up. "Yeah, right." She kept on eating but after a few moments of silence, she looked at Jake and realized he was serious. She stared in disbelief, trying to find truth in his statement. Was it possible? For several moments she examined his face. Slowly, she started to see it. Shave clean the salt & pepper beard stubble, darken and lengthen the hair, pull it back into the famous chef's signature ponytail that always reached to the middle of his back, remove a few wrinkles and sitting before her was...Chef J, celebrity chef to the stars who disappeared several years ago, never to be heard from again! People couldn't figure out where he went or why he stopped cooking. He was just gone, making way for less talented but more ambitious chefs to move up in the ranks and fill the space he vacated. Realizing she probably looked like a star-struck schoolgirl, she finally blurted out, "But you're famous!"

He chuckled. "So are you."

"Not like you! You were *the* celebrity chef. People made reservations months in advance at your restaurants. I know because my parents tried to take me to one for my high school graduation. We had to wait until August and that was when you were fairly new! I can still taste the Beef Wellington melting in my mouth."

"One of my specialties. But it seems like a lifetime since I've made it."

Sue still couldn't quite believe it. "You were everywhere. Every time your name was in the entertainment news you were cooking for someone even more famous. You cooked for Presidents!" She couldn't help but sound star-struck. "Then you disappeared."

"I didn't disappear. I left and moved to a ranch in Montana. Since Mary was my manager and nobody knew my real name, it was easy to slip away without a trace. We sold all the businesses and bought this ranch. I cut my hair, started going by my full name and built a whole new life for me and my family."

"But why? You had it all. At least, that's the way it seemed."

"Don't believe the hype! I got tired of being the 'Chef To The Stars' and cooking for people who were unbelievably self-absorbed and only cared about impressing their friends by doing things like having me cater their pretentious parties. I swear, at a certain point I could have made mac and cheese with a box mix and clients would have swooned over it like I created a new delicacy just for them. It was disgusting!" Jake found himself getting anxious just thinking about his former life as a celebrity chef. But at the same time, being honest about the past and talking about it with Sue made him feel...content. "Coming here was the best thing I could have done for my sanity."

She was still trying to process everything she had just been told. "But going from being a world-renowned chef to being a cattle rancher seems like quite an untenable leap."

"Not when I grew up on a ranch. I had a very well-rounded upbringing. Got my love of animals and ranching from my Dad and my love of cooking from my Mom. Since one love had served me well and basically set me up for life, I decided to see how the other love would serve me. So far, I'm happy with the results." *Except where my family is concerned.* But he decided to see how Sue reacted to his first bombshell before delving into that mess.

They ate in silence for a few minutes as the storm howled outside. Sue thought about how Jake had done so much in his lifetime and about what he had just told her and it started to make sense. The life of a celebrity chef, or any celebrity for that matter, most likely wasn't as easy and glamorous as the media made it appear. She admired him for making such a drastic change in his life for the sake of the ones he loved. She looked up from her now mostly empty plate. "You're very fortunate Jake. Most people don't get to follow their passion even once in their lives and you've been able to do it twice. You've very blessed."

Jake swallowed his last bite as he contemplated what she had said. "I never really thought of it that way but you're right. My parents inspired me to achieve the goals I set for myself and instilled a passion in me for two things that have taken me far in life. Everyone should be so fortunate."

"Perhaps that's why you help others so much." He gave her a puzzled look at which she smiled. "While I haven't specifically been doing research on you, I couldn't help but come to learn how much you do for the town. Everyone I talked to had a story to tell about things you've done for the community, for individuals. It's clear you care and I hope you know how much people appreciate it."

He didn't know how to respond without sounding pretentious. He did like helping people but he never thought about why. If he had given it any thought he would have attributed his generosity to the lessons his parents taught him but had he examined it further, he might have to admit it likely had more to do with the failed relationship he had with his own kids. If he couldn't help them, he'd help others.

They were silent again as they absorbed the thoughts generated by their conversation. Sue's hunger was more than satisfied as she savored the last morsel from her plate and sat back. "That was amazing! Thank you so much."

"My pleasure. Felt good to cook again. Dolly only lets me near the kitchen when I follow her instructions to the letter!" He paused as he shot Sue a satisfied smile. "Hope you left room for dessert. I noticed Dolly made one of her specialties while we were gone. Chocolate Peppermint Mousse. It's highly recommended by this chef!"

"How can I resist? But I may need to let this meal settle for a bit first."

"Agreed," he declared as he patted his stomach. "Let's go into the great room and sit in front of the fire for a bit. Dessert isn't going anywhere." They rose from their chairs and moved into the other room with Bernie close behind, looking forward to curling up by the fire and resting after his busy day.

As they entered the room where the tree they had cut down only days before was glowing with lights and decorations, Sue was taken back to her childhood by the smell of freshly cut pine. She hadn't realized it before just then but it had been years since the scent she enjoyed so much in her youth had even been noticed in her adulthood. "Trees don't smell anymore," she said as much to herself as to anyone listening.

"What's that?" Jake asked as he headed towards the stereo to put on some music.

Lost in her thoughts, Sue realized she had made the comment out loud. "Sorry, I just realized that trees don't smell anymore. It's been years since I walked into a room and smelled the fresh scent of pine."

Jake nodded. "That's because the trees you get in the city were cut down long before you take one home. The longer a tree has been cut, the less moisture there is inside so the sap which contains the scent dries up and the scent gets locked inside the wood. A freshly cut tree that's kept in water will fill a room with its scent for quite a while. I imagine the last tree you had that smelled was one your family cut down." He held up some CDs in his hands. "Any requests?"

He was right. But cutting down a tree was something that hadn't been a Christmas ritual for too many years to count. Before she allowed herself to wallow in forgotten memories, she responded. "I'm good with listening to the music of the wind."

He beamed with delight. "Spoken like a true cowgirl!"

They sat together in front of the fireplace and watched the flames dance as they listened to the storm. Sue looked out the massive window to confirm her suspicion that the snow was continuing to fall with an intensity she wasn't certain she had ever witnessed. Eventually, she couldn't help herself. "So how did you decide to move out here?"

"We actually came to this part of Montana during one of the rare vacations we took. Fell in love with the area immediately, probably in part because people out here didn't really know who I was. Or care! But the move never would have happened if Mary hadn't suggested we get out of the city in the first place. Once the option was out there, it became more and more obvious to me that it made sense to not only move out of the city but to also change the course of my life...our lives. We talked about it a lot before making the decision. I wanted to be sure we could make a real go of it here. We had enough money to get started but if the ranch turned out to be a money pit, I'd have to start all over again as a chef. When we finally decided to take the plunge, things happened quickly. And before long, we were doing pretty well out here. And no one cared about my former life. Guess they don't follow the whole 'celebrity chef' thing in the heartland. They have more important things to concentrate on! Folks just accepted us as new ranchers who seemed to know what we were doing so that successfully ingratiated us to the local community. No one ever really asked where we came from."

"From the conversations I've had with the people of Spruce, it seems they have nothing but positive things to say about you. And they have particularly good things to say about the holiday events you host."

"Mary loved hosting parties, which is how we got to know the locals when we first arrived. And it's how the vacation thing started. She loved doing things for others. When she got sick, I tried to get her to slow down and I wanted to stop the vacations. But she wouldn't hear of it. She felt that as long as she had energy to do it, she would. And if she could do something extra to make a holiday special for someone, it was worth the time she'd have to spend resting afterwards."

"I'm sure she'd be pleased you continue to host vacationers."

"I'd like to think so but we don't do them as much as we did when she was alive. Mostly we do them a few weeks in the summer and for some holidays."

"Wayne told me about the special cancer patient event you host on the 4th of July."

Jake smiled. "Yeah, he loves that one."

"It's a beautiful tribute to your wife, who was obviously the rock in your life."

Jake stared as the fire thinking about the truth of Sue's statement. He had never spoken with anyone in detail about Mary since her passing but it felt good. Sue seemed to appreciate what they had and recognized the importance of Mary in his life. Theirs was a true partnership. He doubted he'd ever find such an equal relationship ever again. Not that he was necessarily looking. But somehow Sue gave him hope he might find it again one day.

"I hope you don't mind me asking but do your kids come to visit often or help with the holiday events?"

Finally, it had arrived, the topic of discussion he didn't want but knew was coming. After avoiding it for so long, on the precipice of the dreaded conversation taking place, he was surprisingly calm. His matter-of-fact response conveyed his regret and disappointment. "They don't ever come here."

Sue immediately regretted asking. She had sensed the first time he mentioned his kids that they were a sore point in his life and JoAnne's comments about them seemed to confirm her first impression. To Sue's surprise though, Jake offered an explanation.

"They were teenagers when we moved here, leaving behind a very comfortable life. But we decided to make the change because we knew my celebrity status was exposing them to some unhealthy habits and if we didn't do something about it, we'd regret it, big time! We'd seen friends and families ruined by drugs and alcohol and other addictions that were rampant in the lifestyle we were entrenched in. Mary and I couldn't allow it to adversely affect our family so we got as far away from it as we could. But the kids hated being here and had no issue with letting us know it whenever they could. They liked the life we had left behind, hanging with celebrities, getting special treatment wherever we went, all that crap that was not normal. They got spoiled and naturally they resented us for taking them away from everything they enjoyed. We tried to explain that we were making the change *for* them, to *help* them, to keep them safe in a healthier environment. Of course, they didn't see it that way because teenagers know everything. Just ask them!" Jake felt himself getting worked up talking about his ungrateful children and felt embarrassed laying out his family's shortcomings to Sue. But he didn't see any reason to hold back. He felt comfortable talking with her. "Anyway, they couldn't wait to leave here and when it was time for college, that's just what they did. They both choose schools that were far away and they never came back. Then when Mary got sick, they blamed me."

Shock overtook Sue and before she could stop herself, she blurted out her indignation. "That's ridiculous! They can't blame you for her getting sick!" And just as quickly, she recognized that she had completely overstepped her bounds. "I'm so sorry Jake. It's certainly not my place to comment on these type of family matters."

He waved his hand to convey the apology was unnecessary. "Of course, they didn't blame me for her *getting* sick. But they were angry I wouldn't move back to the city so she could get better treatment. Kids may think they have all the answers but they rarely do. Mary and I talked to the best specialists and there just wasn't anything that could be done. They all said that, as long as she was happy and content, that was the best medicine for her. Sometimes the mind can help more than medicine. I know that if I had taken her back to the city, she would have been miserable and passed sooner. She simply didn't want to die anywhere but here. So we stayed. Doctors gave her 6 months. She lasted almost 2 years."

Sue stared at the fire as she quietly spoke. "Proof that she was most likely happy to the very end."

"I truly believe she was. She told me that every day out here was a blessing for her. But when she took a bad turn near Christmas, the kids couldn't get here in time to say goodbye."

"I'm so sorry Jake. I know that had to be difficult for them." Unfortunately, Sue indeed had experience in such matters but certainly didn't want to get into the particulars at the moment. Nothing she could say about what happened to her parents would help.

"Their busy lives were the reason they didn't get to say goodbye...but again, they blamed me." Sue could sense the growing frustration he was feeling at reliving an ugly part of his past. "We moved out here to show them they didn't need to live like that. We wanted them to understand there is more to life than worrying about moving up the corporate ladder and impressing others and meeting deadlines. Guess we failed." Then it occurred to him who he was talking with. "Sorry, no disrespect intended. I know you have a deadline looming. But we wanted them to know they had a choice. They were so wrapped up in their lives they couldn't see the forest for the trees!"

It was obvious that Jake felt strongly about the decisions he and Mary made together and believed those choices were what was best for their family. "You know you did what was best for your wife and they should be able to see that, especially now as adults."

"You would think so. But they haven't been back here or spoken to me since the funeral."

Again they sat in silence, watching the flames, reflecting on their conversation. To Sue, it seemed he was surprisingly well-adjusted to all that had transpired. However, she couldn't help but wonder how Jake seemed to easily get through the Christmas holiday when it was the time of year that he lost his beloved wife. She didn't think she could have looked at any holiday with a positive attitude if her parents had been taken from her on or close to one. "Can I ask you a personal question?"

Jake nodded as he continued to stare at the fire, hoping she wasn't going to ask for more details about his kids.

She chose her words carefully so as not to imply anything improper. "You seem to enjoy Christmas time, preparing for the party, decorating, tree hunting. But since Mary passed just as the holiday was approaching, I'm thinking that would make the holiday difficult for you. How do you maintain such an upbeat attitude on such a sad anniversary?"

It took a few moments for him to formulate his response. He, too, wanted to choose the right words to correctly explain how he managed what Sue correctly assumed would be a difficult time. He loved Mary and kept her memory alive and never wanted to seem as though he had forgotten one moment of their life together. "It's actually fairly simple. I think of all the good times and don't dwell on the bad." He finally broke his stare at the fire, looking at Sue as he explained further. "A lot of people dwell on the anniversary of losing a loved one, becoming down when that anniversary occurs. But I choose to remember the good times that happened prior to the bad. Mary and I had many good years and I have plenty of fun memories to dwell on rather than thinking about the sadness I felt at the end. So, to get past that, I think of all the positives that Mary brought into my life. I wouldn't be the man I am today without having known her."

"But you make it sound easier than I'm certain it is. She loved Christmas but her passing at such a festive season seems likely to contradict what we feel at this time of year."

"Or, you can look at it as something that makes perfect sense. She loved Christmas so what better time for God to call her to heaven?" He could tell Sue was having a hard time understanding what he was trying to tell her and finally thought of a better way to explain himself. "Her mother's favorite holiday was New Year's and *Auld Lang Syne* was her favorite song. Her mother always looked at the holiday as a new beginning, a time to dismiss whatever bad had happened throughout the previous year."

"I feel the same way. It's basically a holiday made to celebrate new beginnings."

"And Mary's mother died on New Year's Eve."

Sue stared at him blankly, taking in what he had just told her.

"But Mary never looked at New Year's Eve as a sad reminder. To the contrary, she always looked at the holiday as a good time to reflect and remember the goodness that was her mother. It made sense to her that her mother died on her favorite holiday so Mary always appreciated the celebration of New Year's, in memory of her mother."

Sue looked into Jake's eyes for several moments taking in the wisdom he just articulated. Then she felt as though if she looked at him one second more, she might burst into tears. She turned to watch the fire again, wishing that someone had told her what he just did when the first anniversary of her parent's murder occurred. It had brought back thoughts of hurt and anger and she couldn't shake her sadness for days afterwards. Would it have made a difference if on that day someone had told her what Jake just said? She wasn't sure. But she felt certain it would have helped her to cope throughout her life. Remembering the positives instead of dwelling on the negatives seemed so logical and made so much sense. She wished she had realized this simple truth long ago.

For several minutes, the silence in the room was only disturbed by the crackling fire and the howling wind. "I want to thank you for sharing that wisdom with me. It's a beautiful way to look at everything. But I feel I've managed to bring down an otherwise lovely evening so for that I am very sorry."

Jake dismissed her apology. "Don't worry about it. Feels good to talk about everything after all this time. Cathartic." He wasn't sure why he had never talked to anyone about that part of his life before. Perhaps it was due to the fact that his kids had embarrassed him for years with their entitled behavior and he felt talking about the manner in which they handled their mother's death would just pile on more embarrassment. "But I'm thinking dessert is just what's needed to get this evening back on track!" With a wink, he got up, put more wood on the fire and quickly walked to the kitchen to dish out the tasty treat that was awaiting them.

*****

"This is amazing!" From the moment Sue tasted the dessert Jake had served, she couldn't stop eating it. In all her travels she had never tasted anything quite like it. "Is this one of your recipes?"

"Apparently you didn't follow my career as obsessively as others!" He had never been a dessert chef. But he always had a good one at each of his restaurants and worked with the best when he was catering a celebrity party. "This delectable delight is the brainchild of our very own Dolly. I've never met someone so creative with desserts."

"Come on now. No offence to Dolly but I find that hard to believe. I can't imagine you didn't always have the best desserts at functions you catered."

"Oh I had plenty of fancy desserts at my functions. Frilly things with edible gold that looked gorgeous but were nothing special in the taste department. Dolly makes things that don't look all that fancy but are satisfying to the soul."

"'Desserts that satisfy the soul'. Sounds like a good name for an article," Sue mused. As she finished off the mousse, she made a mental note to ask Dolly for the recipe.

"So I have to ask. How did a woman who is such a natural on a horse became a travel writer? Why didn't you become your family's first cowgirl?"

Sue hadn't talked about the twists and turns of her life in years. No one ever asked. But then, not many people knew of her youthful dreams. "I loved riding when I was young. Couldn't get enough of it, the feeling I got when I was on a horse!" The gleam in her eyes said as much as the words she spoke. "Rode as much as I could, competed in rodeos and got especially good at barrel racing. But in high school I started writing for the school newspaper. People told me I had a knack for it so in my senior year, I took a creative writing course to better learn the process and discovered I had a passion for it as well. I seem to have a way with words that people relate to. So, I decided to make my living writing instead of sweating it out on a ranch or in a rodeo."

"Just like that? Seems like you took as much of a left-turn as I did."

"Pretty much. But like yours, my parents instilled a passion in me that inspired my path in life. Traveling at a young age sparked something in me that has served me well." Sue never regretted her choice. The last couple weeks confirmed what she knew when she decided to change the course of her future. Life on a ranch is a lot of work. And she knew that not all ranches were managed the way Wayne ran The Big M. She had made the right choice years ago. But the last few weeks also informed her that something was missing in her life.

"Have you always written your travel articles or have you written anything I might have
read?"

She feigned great indignity. "What?!? You don't read travel blogs and magazines constantly?"

He smiled. "Hard to believe, I know."

"Out of college I wrote for a local newspaper while I started on the 'next great American novel'."

"I'm impressed. How did it turn out?"

"I'd love to tell you it was a best-seller but I'd have to finish it first. So while the novel wasn't happening, I started to get noticed for a blog I had started and one thing lead to another until I found myself writing a column for the top travel magazine in the country. I'm still not sure how it happened but it seems like yesterday that I was struggling to write my book."

"What was it about?"

"Oh, I had come up with a riveting storyline. Boy meets girl, they fall in love, they have a falling out, a friend explains how stupid they are being, they get back together and they end up living happily ever after. Sound unique?"

"Hmmm, not sure but I think I saw that in a movie once."

She chuckled knowingly. "Me too, more than once. I just couldn't come up with an original story, some twist to make it stand out. So I never saw the point in writing it. But writing about travel is such a breeze. The right words seem to fall out of my fingers onto the keyboard so that my readers are intrigued to explore the places I visit."

"Well then, it sounds like you've found your place in the world."

Sue glanced at Jake with an expression that asked what he meant.

"Do you like what you do?"

"Very much."

"Does it help others?"

"I hope it does. I think it does."

"Are you satisfied?"

The honest answer to that question was a little harder for Sue to express. With her work she was very satisfied. She had the freedom to write what she wanted and a supportive editor. She had tremendously supportive friends whom she could count on in any situation. However, satisfaction on a more intimate level was another story. But since Jake was seemingly referring to her professional career, her answer finally came in a nod.

Jake noted her hesitation but continued without questioning her. "Then you're fortunate enough to have found your place in, and contribute to, the world around you."

"Oh, I think you attribute too much importance to what I do. I just write articles that hopefully inspire people to get out and see different places. Don't know that it's any kind of great contribution to mankind or anything."

"And that is where you are underestimating your worth. Think about it! People seek out destinations because they have read the unique details you describe in your articles and they want to see and experience them for themselves, see the beauty you saw, taste the foods you enjoyed, meet the local people. Think of the businesses you've helped by inspiring people to travel to their cities and towns. Think of the joy you've helped people experience who never would have gone somewhere if it wasn't for your articles. That's a gift. Lots of people never find something that truly fulfills them *and* helps others."

Sue looked at Jake with appreciation as she came to the realization he was right. She had never thought of her career as particularly helpful to mankind but everything he said made sense. And if she needed proof, she had only to think of JoAnne, who professed to Sue only days earlier that the articles she read gave birth to a growing desire in her to travel. "It seems we are both fortunate enough to have found our proper places in the world."

CHAPTER 13

Jake usually rose with the sun but after the cattle drive and late dinner with Sue, he struggled to remove himself from his warm, comfortable bed. The lack of sun streaming through his window told him the snow was likely still falling but it seemed as though the wind had mercifully subsided. He knew Wayne would be on top of what needed to be done but knowing there was still plenty to do as a result of the storm, he forced himself to get up. Once dressed, he passed by Sue's room and didn't hear her stirring. She was either still asleep or working on her article. Either way, he decided it was best not to disturb her.

The smell of bacon drew him to the kitchen. He always appreciated that Dolly had fresh, crispy bacon waiting for him no matter what time he came down for breakfast. "Morning!"

"Any later and you'd be sayin' 'afternoon'!" she chided him.

"What can I say?" He clutched his lower back and adopted an exaggerated limp as he 'struggled' to make it to the table. "I'm an old man who needs his rest."

Dolly rolled her eyes as she placed a plate of scrambled eggs, bacon and toast in front of him. "You need to age about 30 years before you're 'old'."

"Have you talked to Wayne?"

"They're starting to clear the snow from the paths and driveway."

Jake nodded, knowing that even with the snow still falling, getting a start on moving it now would make things easier later. "Have you seen Sue this morning?"

"I heard her stirring earlier but nothing since."

Jake ate his breakfast in silence as he reflected on the previous evening's conversation. He never talked about his kid's resentment of the situation they had seen as hastening their mother's passing. They literally screamed at Jake the last time he saw them. They couldn't comprehend the fact that Mary wanted to stay at the ranch and they were certain Jake was lying to them about what the doctors had said. But he wasn't going to force something on Mary that she didn't want, no matter how much their kids pushed. He had hoped that as they grew older and wiser, they might come to realize he only did what their mother wanted. But every year that went by without a phone call, a letter or maybe a surprise appearance at the annual Christmas party told him they simply hadn't matured enough yet to understand. The decision to move to the ranch in the first place had been driven by Mary and Jake's desire for their kids to grow up in a more normal environment where they could understand and appreciate hard work and the rewards it provided rather than being indulged by his celebrity status. He never regretted the move or the decision to stay once Mary got sick. But he did miss his, apparently still self-centered, kids.

*****

It was getting hard for Sue to ignore her grumbling stomach or the smell of bacon wafting from the kitchen but she was determined to get her article finished before going down for breakfast. She had been awake since just before dawn. As the sun tried to brighten the cloudy morning sky, she realized she no longer heard the howling wind. She arose and looked out the window to see snow still falling steadily but not as heavy as when she went to bed. Maybe there was hope the roads would be open later in the day. She lay down again but couldn't get back to sleep, her conversation with Jake the previous evening playing over and over in her head. She couldn't help but be saddened at the situation between him and his kids. JoAnne had made it clear she didn't think much of them and it sounded like they didn't give Jake credit for being someone who only had their Mother's best interest at heart. *Why do kids think they know everything?* Her mind started to wander and, even though there were cowboys and cowgirls and house staff at the ranch, thoughts of Jake being alone started to generate all manner of notions in her head. *OK, time to get up and get to work!* She quickly dressed, then opened her laptop, knowing her rapidly approaching deadline and the unfinished article would get her mind back on track. She wanted to finish before noon and was determined to do so.

Sue read what she had written so far. Then she checked her notes and started working from the beginning, inserting details she had missed. While her original plans for the story were to only talk about cowboys and cowgirls and their holiday traditions, the article had taken on a new profile over the course of her research. She realized that the ranch and the people who worked there were an important part of the local community and, while Jake was the mainstay and inspiration, everyone on the ranch helped the town. She had been told story after story to prove the point. Whether it was helping to repair the leaking library roof or inviting the townsfolk to the ranch the Sunday after Thanksgiving for a bull roast to help get everyone in the Christmas spirit, Jake and his people had a big impact on the town. So it was only fitting that Sue work details about the town itself into her article. The hardworking residents; the businesses; the festival; they all became part of it along with her original idea. The article was now much more than a rundown of cowboy Christmas traditions and it felt right to her.

She proofread her article and realized she didn't have the strong closing it needed. As she scoured her notes for something to provide the ending she wanted, she recalled Jake had said something the night they sat by the fire pit which had made a significant impression on her. She kept looking through her notes to find the quote and realized she hadn't taken notes that evening. They were simply conversing. She tried for several long moments to recall exactly what he had said. Finally, her fingers flew across the keyboard as it came to her and she wrote the last lines of her article before the words she had been searching for fell out of her head! 'When cowboys are lucky enough to be tending their herd on Christmas night, out on the peaceful range, the music of the wind in the trees, a crackling fire to keep them warm and serenity all around them, they need only to look up and see that they have more Christmas lights to enjoy than anyone. And on Christmas, the stars shine just a little bit brighter.'

Done! Finally! Sue was satisfied she had accomplished what she set out to do when she developed the idea for her Christmas article as she attached it to an e-mail addressed to the magazine's webmaster and her editor, just in time for it to be proof-read and posted the next day. And Sue always sent her articles to Jackie and Melanie when they were finished. They were her biggest supporters and she enjoyed sharing her work with them before the general public.

*****

With the weight of finishing the article off her shoulders, Sue went into the kitchen to get some breakfast, although it was almost lunchtime! As she moved through the great room, Jake was coming in from the porch. "Morning sleepyhead! I thought I might have to come in and throw a snowball at you."

"I've been up since 5:30 smarty."

"Watching for the snow to stop so you could build a snow fort?"

"I wish! Haven't done that since I was a kid. But I couldn't sleep any longer with the looming deadline so I worked on my article."

"I trust that the satisfied look on your face indicates it's done."

"Indeed it is. Just sent it to my editor who is, no doubt, very happy to get it a day early. He hates it when I cut things close."

"Guess that's my fault. I kept you out here longer than you planned and then the storm really messed things up. But I have to say I really enjoyed having you on the tree hunt and you were a huge help getting the herd back here so I'm not sorry." Last night's conversation somehow made Jake see Sue in a new light.

"No need to be sorry. I could have left days ago but I've been having so much fun I just never wanted to leave." A truer statement she hadn't made in quite some time.

"Well, Wayne was right yesterday. You ever get tired of being a city girl, you can be a cowgirl here."

"Don't tempt me! I've felt more alive these past couple weeks than I have in years." This was yet another very true statement! "I could get used to this."

"I'm serious. I'll take a cowgirl like you anytime!"

They looked at each other for several moments, each realizing there was more being said in their conversation than the words that were spoken. Jake wondered if he was ready for more than the solitary life he had been leading. And Sue wondered if perhaps she had taken the right path in her life after all. Or maybe it was simply time for a change, like the one he had made. They were both thankful that before things between them got too awkward, Dolly emerged from the kitchen. "Who wants breakfast and who wants lunch?"

*****

"Thanks so much for helping with my last minute shopping!" Jackie and Mark had just returned to her apartment, loaded with bags of food and gifts.

Mark smiled and bowed. "My pleasure madam. But why did you buy so much food? Thought it was just us for Christmas."

"And your sister! I'm looking forward to meeting her and she's coming all the way from Chicago so I want to make sure she has a nice first Christmas here!"

"Yeah, but she's staying with me. You have enough food here to feed us all for a week!"

"You can't honestly think I'm not cooking dinner for her while she's here, do you? Probably more than once." Even though they hadn't been together long, Jackie knew Mark was no chef!

He shrugged. "Figured we'd eat out."

"Men know nothing about entertaining guests!" she laughed. "Don't suppose you want to stick around and help me wrap everything?" She was certain he would rather do anything else than wrap presents but tried to entice him anyway with a wink. "I'll make it worth your while."

"I suppose I can at least help put the groceries away if you bribe me with some eggnog. But you don't want me anywhere near wrapping paper. The only thing I can do with it is rip it off gifts!"

"Fair enough. I'll spike the eggnog if you'll get me the spiced rum from above the fridge."

He was eager to comply. He had never used spiced rum in eggnog before but it sounded good. As he grabbed the bottle, he heard the sound of a horse whinny. "What was that?!?"

Jackie laughed as she took her phone out of her purse. "I changed the alert sound for messages from Sue to a horse while she's researching her story. Figured it was appropriate." She read the message and squealed with delight. "Her article is done!"

"Cool. She got it in ahead of the deadline. Her research must have gone well."

"I'll soon find out. She sent Melanie and I the article."

"Can you send it to me? I'd love to not have to wait until it's posted to read it."

He finished putting away the food while she prepared the drinks, then they settled into the couch and each opened the article on their phones. They read in silence as Jackie smiled to herself. She was glad that Sue seemed to have found a good source but was also happy to see that her friend hadn't completely given up on her standard fare, writing about the town as much as she did about what cowboys and cowgirls do at Christmas. It seemed to Jackie the article was a good balance of the "old" Sue and the new thoughts she was looking to incorporate.

At the same time, Mark read the same words with a different reaction. His face belied his thoughts as his expression went from blank to puzzled to disbelief.

As Jackie finished reading, she saw Mark turn off his phone and knew he was done as well. "I enjoyed that very much! I really didn't know if her subject choice would work but I shouldn't have been worried. Sue's a magician with words." She turned to him to get his reaction. But instead of appearing happy for a job well done by his co-worker, she saw a look of sadness and loneliness covering his face. She wasn't sure but she thought he might have been trembling. "Are you OK? You look as if you've seen a ghost!"

Mark stared blankly at his phone screen for several long moments, still comprehending what he had read. Finally, he got up and walked to the bedroom. "Excuse me. I need to make a phone call."

Behind the closed bedroom door, he punched numbers on his phone. After a few rings, a familiar female voice came on. "Don't tell me you're calling to cancel Christmas! I'm packing now!" She always enjoyed teasing her brother about his unique talent for coming up with last minute excuses to get out of something. But he wasn't in the mood to joke with her now.

"I'm going to send you an article and you need to read it immediately. It was written by a co-worker whom I suggested should go to Montana to research cowboys." He paused, not believing what he was about to say. "I think we need to take a trip."

CHAPTER 14

Jake was putting on his coat as Sue came from the kitchen after helping Dolly clean up. "Heading down to see Wayne?"

He nodded as he sat down to put on his boots. "Figure I should get a report on whatever issues the storm caused and how soon he expects to have the driveway and parking area cleared. Guests will hopefully be arriving in a few days. And I'm assuming you'll be wanting to get out of here as soon as everything is cleared." Her leaving wasn't something he was looking forward to but hoped his expression didn't give him away.

Truth be told, she had been giving her leaving much consideration. She realized that since she had been spending time at The Big M, hunting for trees, helping with the cattle drive, getting to know Jake and understand everything that went on at the ranch, she felt contentment in her life; a peace she hadn't known for quite some time. The odd thing was, she hadn't realized anything was wrong in her life before coming to the ranch. She loved her job and didn't want to do anything else. But something about being around animals again, away from the craziness of the city and the constant demands it imposed, told her that something *was* missing in her life. And if she couldn't exactly change her situation, she could at least hold on to what was making her feel so content for as long as she could. She was hesitant to ask but took a deep breath and started talking before she lost her nerve. "Well, I was actually thinking of taking you up on your offer and staying here a little while longer, help you get ready for the Christmas Eve party and maybe see what all the excitement is about." She became nervous that perhaps he hadn't really been sincere when he suggested she stay after they got back from the drive.

Jake tried to play it cool. "As far as I'm concerned, you can stay as long as you like." And he couldn't resist teasing her. "Are you sure all that shopping and baking and decorating you *have* to do before Christmas can wait? Or not get done at all if you stay long enough?"

Sue looked at him for several moments, his hopeful smile speaking volumes. Her appreciation of him seemingly grew every moment they were together. "I'm starting to rethink my priorities."

This was music to his ears. "Glad to hear it. And grateful to have the help. We lost a day in party-prep dealing with the herd so check in with Dolly to see what needs to be done here while I go see Wayne." Now it was Jake whose appreciation was growing. Sue's presence had brought a brightness to the ranch that hadn't existed since Mary's passing. They were certainly two totally different people. But he realized the house felt happier when Sue was around.

*****

Sue watched from the window as Jake made his way towards the barn. It appeared that Wayne already had the path from the house clear and now the parking area was being worked on and the driveway clearing had started as well. Thankfully, the snowfall had slowed a bit. But it was clear to her that Jake's prediction it would be a day or two before she could even attempt to leave was accurate. And while she had been planning all along to be home by now, she was starting to feel happy that she wasn't. And she realized this was incredibly unusual. Typically if she was traveling at Christmas, she would get more uptight and anxious the longer she was away from home. But not this year. And the realization that she was missing out on so many "important" things like helping Melanie find a tree and shopping with Jackie and baking with both of them didn't faze her. It was very unlike her to be so content at Christmas when she wasn't home. She truly didn't know if it was the ranch, the animals, the people she had met...or something else. She just knew that she felt more content in the previous two weeks than she had felt in a long, long time and she knew that she wanted the feeling to last as long as possible. And while she hadn't specifically said she might stay through Christmas, she did say she wanted to see what all the excitement was about with the Christmas cowboy vacationers and the annual Christmas Eve party. Thankfully, Jake didn't seem at all fazed by the notion of her staying through the holiday. The article was done and in reality, there was real reason for her to go home.

Except she had to break the news to her best friends. Their holiday traditions varied over the years, depending on work schedules and each other's availability. But ever since they had all become close, they always had a nice, long, relaxing Christmas Eve Brunch at the Ritz. Each of them looked forward to it and none of them had ever missed it. This year Sue would be the first one of them to break the tradition. This was the only disadvantage of her decision to stay at the ranch. But with Christmas Eve only a few days away, she had to let her friends know. She decided to call Jackie first. After only one ring, she answered. "You're not going to be happy with me."

"I'm already not happy with you!"

This wasn't at all the response Sue had been expecting. "What do you mean? I haven't even told you my bad news yet."

"Oh, I already figured out that if you weren't home by now, you weren't going to make it for brunch this year."

"And how did you come to that conclusion?"

"Since we haven't heard from you, Melanie and I figured there's something there that's more interesting than us. But don't sweat it. We all knew it would happen sooner or later."

"What would happen?" Sue was having trouble following their conversation.

"One of us had to fall in love sooner or later and would eventually bail on our holiday traditions. And quite honestly, I was thinking it might be me this year. But thanks to your article, that ain't happening."

"OK, first of all, I'm not bailing on our traditions because I'm in love. Well, not like you're thinking. But I do love it here and I'm actually feeling relaxed for the first time in years. I'm not sure what's happened to me but I like it." Or maybe she knew more than she wanted to let on to Jackie. Or Melanie. Or herself. "But I don't know what my article has to do with me bailing on brunch. What's going on?"

Jackie realized she had to slow down and fill in some blanks. "OK, I don't blame your article...or you. But ever since Mark read it, he's acting weird."

"Weird how?'

"When you sent me the link, I shared it with him. I know I'm not supposed to show your articles to anyone but I figured he works with you so it wouldn't matter. Anyway, as soon as he was done reading it, he had this odd look, like he remembered something and was in trouble. Next thing I know, instead of his sister coming here, the two of them have to go somewhere Christmas Eve."

"Christmas Eve?!? Why then specifically?"

"I have no idea. His sister had been planning to come here for Christmas and I was excited to meet her, thinking it was a good sign for us. I had all these plans to make a nice dinner but now they have to go somewhere else. Says it's a family event he hasn't been to in years and he'll explain when he gets back. I didn't even know he had family besides his sister! Haven't seen him since the night he read the article." Jackie's frustration and sadness was evident as her voice started to crack. "Now I don't know what's going on between us."

Sue's heart ached for her friend. Hearing only Jackie's perspective, she couldn't exactly figure out what happened but she intended to talk to Mark when she got back to the office.

She didn't take kindly to someone hurting her friend and would never have introduced them if she hadn't thought Mark to be a decent guy. But this didn't sound like something a "decent" guy did. *He better have a good excuse!* "I'm really sorry Jackie. I don't really know Mark all that well but maybe he has trouble with commitment. Maybe the thought of introducing you to his family became too much for him."

"But it was his idea to invite her for Christmas! I've been very careful not to be too clingy and all that. We seemed to be getting along so well. Now I'm just scared. I really liked him."

"I know. I can tell. But let's not jump to any conclusions. You said he told you he would explain when he gets back. So that's a good sign. Maybe something came up that's too personal for him to talk about right now. You told me he doesn't like to talk about his past and you two have only been dating a month so see what he has to say when he returns and go from there."

"Guess I don't really have a choice." The defeat in her voice was obvious but it was mixed with a glimmer of hope. "Anyway, don't worry about me. You have fun with your cowboy and maybe he'll let you out of his lasso in time for New Year's."

Thank God! Jackie still had some of her wit! "He's not the reason I'm staying."

"Uh huh. I believe you." Sarcasm practically dripped out of the phone.

Sue couldn't help but smile. "OK, not the *only* reason. This place is special. Maybe one day you'll get to see for yourself. If things work out, you and Mark could book a 'cowboy vacation'!"

"At this point, I'd just like to have a weekend together...anywhere!'

"Don't despair. It'll all work out. I gotta go. You OK?"

"Oh I'm fine, you know me. Takes a lot to keep me down."
"You aren't down. It's just a small bump in the road. I'll call you on Christmas and see you soon." She hung up feeling bad for her friend. Mark definitely had some explaining to do.

*****

With two days left until Christmas Eve, preparations for the annual party and arrival of the guests kicked into high gear. Sue took over the assignment of baking cookies and cakes for the party. She was looking forward to working in such a spacious kitchen. Maneuvering around her tiny one, trying to find space to roll out dough or let cookies cool was an ordeal she was glad to forgo. With counter space that seemed to equal the square footage of her entire apartment and a pantry that was stocked to the ceiling, she enjoyed making treats she hadn't baked for years. She started easy, baking a double batch of chocolate chip cookies, knowing they were always a crowd favorite. But then she branched out and made peanut butter cookies with a chocolate kiss in the middle. Then, a batch of snicker doodles, which she had never made before but when Jake popped his head in to inquire as to whether or not she was planning to make them, Dolly assured her the ingredients were on hand as she dug out her old family recipe, which made a surprisingly chewy cookie with a crisp outer edge. Oatmeal raisin was next and then Sue decided to break out some of her own family recipes. When she was little, her mother would make pecan logs every Christmas. A delicious light, crisp cookie, she had been taught all the secrets to perfecting its unique texture. Then she made her specialty. It was actually her grandmother's specialty, with the recipe passed down to her by her mother.

Baklava was a time consuming project in her grandmother's day. But these days, philo dough was available in most grocery stores, cutting the time it took to make the tasty treat to a fraction of what it took her grandmother. But with no time to get into town and find a store with it in stock, Sue had to resort to making the paper thin dough by hand. She carefully worked to make the dozens of layers of dough she needed, brushing each lightly with melted butter as she layered them into the baking sheet, with finely chopped walnuts layered strategically throughout the assembly process. Cut into diamond shapes and covered with melted butter, Sue was satisfied her grandmother would be proud as she put the tray into the oven and set the timer. Then all she needed to do was make the sweet syrup, which most people mistook for honey, so it could be poured over the pastry as soon as the tray was pulled from the oven. She loved to watch the syrup sizzle as it coated the hot pastry. As she started to prepare the syrup, which involved constant stirring, she finally had a chance to stop and relax a bit while doing nothing more than stirring a pot of slowly boiling liquid.

Sue looked around the massive kitchen, which was a dream come true for someone who loved to cook as much as she did. Even though she knew little about what a kitchen on a typical ranch was like, she knew this one was unique. But now knowing Jake's past, it made perfect sense. She wondered how often he was able to indulge his former profession since he became a rancher. Was the meal he prepared after the cattle drive a regular thing or something that rarely happened? He had indicated it was most likely the latter. And she wondered how much Dolly knew about Jake's former life. He made it sound like nobody knew who he had been but surely *someone* recognized him!

While Sue had been busy baking, Dolly had been steadily working for hours preparing multiple dishes. She made cornbread casseroles, prepared baked beans, and more than one sweet potato casserole. The three ovens in the kitchen would certainly get a workout when everything had to be prepared at the same time on Christmas Eve. And Sue noticed preparation of a particularly delicious looking cornbread casserole she couldn't wait to try! Dolly moved with the precision of someone who knew how to efficiently work a kitchen. As Sue was stirring her syrup, Dolly was expertly cutting up turkey breasts she had baked earlier in the day that had cooled enough to chop for her turkey salad. While they had chatted intermittently through their hours together in the kitchen, they were both finally stationary enough to really converse.

"Dolly, let me know if you need help there. I should be done with this in about 10 minutes according to the timer on my last creation."

"Thanks. But you've been baking like a mad-woman all day. Sure you don't want to take a break?" She was impressed with how Sue had been working non-stop. The wonderful looking creations she was turning out were sure to impress the guests and she appreciated not having to do the baking on top of everything else she was preparing.

"I'm still feeling pretty energized. Working in this kitchen is a breeze. My entire kitchen could fit on the island you're working at!"

Dolly smiled. "I thought you'd have a nice, spacious kitchen back home. You certainly know your way around one."

"As do you. I'm impressed with how much you're able to get done seemingly all at the same time."

"I've been doing this for a while. Started out as a Sous Chef for Jake years ago when he got his first position as an Executive Chef." The expression on Sue's face reflected her surprise that Dolly was revealing something about Jake's past which he seemed interested in keeping under wraps. "He told me about your conversation the other night."

"Thank goodness!" Sue's relief was evident in her voice. "I wasn't sure who knew about him."

"More people know than you might think, although I'm pretty sure JoAnne doesn't because she's still trying to figure out how Jake makes such moist ham biscuits."

"Ham biscuits? I haven't heard anything about them yet!"

"He makes 'em every year for Christmas. Says they're a cowboy tradition but I have no clue where he got that idea. And I have no idea what his secret is. He says if he tells me he'd have to shoot me. Mostly he just likes to tease me about knowing something I don't." Dolly smiled as she spoke fondly of her old friend. "Anyway, people that know about his past don't let on because they just don't care. He's become part of this community, simple as that. People in these parts don't care about celebrity stuff. Jake is genuine and down-to-earth. That's what people care about."

Sue was glad to hear there were still some places where celebrities didn't hold much sway. To her, celebrity-worship had gotten way out-of-hand in recent years. "So how did you end up here?"

"Well, like I said, I started out as a Sous Chef but it wasn't long before I was managing Jake's business while Mary managed his career. When he sold the restaurants and decided to come here, I stayed with the business, managing it for the new owners. But it wasn't the same, as you can imagine. Jake was the heart and soul of his restaurants. We still made good food but it wasn't much fun. When I came here to visit and Jake told me he was expanding what they were doing and that Mary wanted to host vacationers looking for the "cowboy experience", he asked if I would come and manage the house staff and business end of things."

"I'm thinking he didn't have to work too hard to convince you."

A broad smile covered Dolly's face. "I'm not even sure he had finished asking me before I said yes! I was getting burned out in the city and I wanted to do something more satisfying. Coming here was the best decision I ever made. And I was glad I was here when Mary got sick. I could help to keep things going while Jake concentrated on her. His kids certainly weren't of any use in that area!"

"He did mention they laid a certain amount of blame at his feet. Seems unjustified."

"That's putting it mildly. They were spoiled coming up but they were old enough to know what was going on and see that there wasn't anything to be done for Mary that would change anything. But they never got over their self-centered selves. I often wonder if they ever matured." The cynicism in Dolly's voice was biting. "They're certainly old enough now that they should have but Jake never hears from them so I guess I have the answer to my question."

The timer for Sue's baklava dinged as she was happy to have a reason to change the conversation. "Ah, it's time for my favorite part!" She carefully took the hot tray from the oven while Dolly looked appreciatively at the golden buttery, nutty delight. Sue placed the tray on the counter then took the slowly boiling pot of syrup from the stove, carefully pouring it evenly as the liquid sizzled immediately upon hitting the hot pastry, confirming it was cooked just right as she smiled with delight.

"I take it that sizzling is a good thing."

"Absolutely. One time I made a pan for my parent's anniversary party and I screwed something up. The syrup didn't sizzle when I poured it. I figured something was wrong but I kept on pouring anyway and sure enough, once everything cooled, it was hard as a rock. Not sure why but the syrup caramelized and I swear I could have constructed a wall with what was in that pan. Had to throw it out and start all over!"

"Been there! Many times!" They laughed as Sue finished up, then started helping Dolly make turkey salad as the food preparations continued.

*****

While food prep was going strong, so were the last minute exterior decorations. Jake supervised the hanging of garland on the porch and stairway while lights were strung along the fence surrounding the house. Fresh wreaths were hung in every window, placed strategically so that the window candle was centered on each wreath. It seemed as though there was a never ending list of things to do but progress was being made. Wayne made sure the team preparing the wagons for the moonlight ride had everything covered and workers continued to move snow and make more room for parked cars. The sunlight was a welcome change in the weather as it helped to dry the pavement and walkways so they didn't freeze at night.

With everything going smoothly outside, Jake went inside to check on the interior preparations. Much of the furniture had already been moved out of the great room and with it out of the way, garland woven with lights was hung from the center of the tall ceiling to the four corners of the room. Once that task was accomplished, chairs were placed around the perimeter of the room and a few standing tables were strategically situated as well.

While the work was being accomplished in the great room, the delicious smells coming from the kitchen enticed Jake to check out progress of the food prep. He knew Dolly would have it under control but he was looking for an excuse to sample some of Sue's baking. He walked into the kitchen as she was arranging cookies on platters and covering them with plastic wrap to keep them fresh. "I don't know that this kitchen has ever produced such enticing baked aromas!"

"Watch your tongue there mister!" Dolly gave him a glare that could kill if she thought for a second he was serious.

Sue enjoyed their playful exchange. The trust that had been built up over years between them was evident. "Careful Cowboy. You could find your chocolate mouse spiked with cyan pepper if you keep that up!"

"She doesn't scare me!" He laughed as he inspected the cookies. "These look delicious. Mind if I sample a few?"

"Just a few. Gotta save them for the guests."

He paused for a second. Mary would always say the same thing when he wanted to dig into the food she was preparing for a party. "Any recommendations?"

"Proper quality control would dictate you try one of each," Sue said with a smile.

"Well, if I must." He prepared himself a selection that would make the cookie monster proud and poured himself a glass of cold milk, then sat at the island to enjoy his sweet afternoon feast.

She appreciated his enthusiasm towards her baking. "Santa would be jealous!"

He had already sampled a few cookies before he ventured a response. "I promise I'll save him some but it might be tough. These are delicious!"

Sue was pleased her baking was a hit, especially with a retired world-renowned chef. Since the flavor in some cookies actually takes a day or two to mature, she knew that certain of her creations would actually be better by the time of the party.

*****

As Christmas Eve arrived, preparations for the party had been accomplished except for one detail. Jake found Sue in the great room playing tug-of-war with Bernie. "Hey you two. Now is not the time to play. We have one more important task to accomplish."

Sue looked up as Bernie continued pulling on his end of the knotted rope. "What could there possibly be left to do? Everything is so festive and decorated to perfection."

Jake smiled wryly. "Not everything. Come on, get your coat on. We have something to take care of outside." He turned to walk towards the mud room. Having heard mention of outside, Bernie quickly dropped the knotted rope and followed.

Once outside, Sue still had no idea what they were about to do as Jake picked up two wreaths propped up at the bottom of the porch steps, handing one to her. "Follow me." They started down the long driveway that Sue had come to know well over the weeks she had been traveling to and from the ranch.

It was finally Christmas Eve and she found herself at peace, enjoying the scenery, the crisp weather, the excitement of the holiday and the company of Jake and Bernie. She went to bed the previous night exhausted from all the work accomplished in preparing for the party but had woken up refreshed and content, a great sense of satisfaction welling up in her. This place was special and to her it didn't matter what Jake had planned for this moment. She was certain it was worth the anticipation.

By the time he stopped walking, they had traversed the entire length of his almost mile-long driveway. "I do this after all the party prep is finished every year. It's my way of telling myself it's time to relax." He took his wreath and hung it in the center of one side of the gate. He looked at Sue and she repeated the ritual on the other gate. "Perfectly done."

They looked at the now properly adorned gate for several moments, then started back towards the house. Even from a distance, one could see the festive atmosphere that was just up ahead. All that was left to do was enjoy the evening.

CHAPTER 15

With most of the travelers checked in and starting to gather in the great room for the annual Christmas Eve party, guests from town started to arrive and the house began to buzz as the festivities got under way. Out-of-town friends caught up with each other and with Jake as he introduced Sue to each of them, explaining her initial mission for visiting the ranch while she explained it was just too wonderful to leave, noting that, much to her chagrin, she'd have to tear herself away sooner rather than later. Everyone she met acknowledged the peaceful feeling the ranch provided and all vowed to check out her blog. But since Jake refused, always with a wink and a smile, to give the wi-fi password to any guests, they'd have to wait until they were home and could get to their computers. Sue noticed that no one complained about not having internet access while at the ranch and several people mentioned it was one of the reasons they traveled there every year. "Totally unplugging for the holiday is a God-send!" was a phrase she heard more than once throughout the evening.

Sue was pleased to see the house come alive with conversation and laughter. She wondered if Jake was sometimes lonely in the huge house when vacationers weren't visiting. She watched him as he conversed with people, seeming to truly enjoy their company. To her, he seemed like a people-person and she imagined that led to his current success but also the success he enjoyed in his previous life. *How difficult it must be for him to be alone all the time* she thought. But she didn't have time to dwell on the thought as he was constantly including her in his conversations.

Jake was impressed with how Sue handled herself in a situation where she knew few of the people surrounding her. Other than the townsfolk she had gotten to know during her stay and his cowboys, she knew no one at the party. Yet she conversed with everyone he introduced her to with ease, able to speak confidently on a number of subjects besides travel. He imagined the ease with which she spoke to strangers helped her immensely in her profession. But he also imagined a person who was so at ease with people might be lonely when she wasn't traveling. However, there wasn't time to dwell on his thoughts as there were guests to be tended to with more arriving.

Dolly was kept busy making sure the food trays stayed full while Jake kept the drinks flowing. Sue took it upon herself to handle the music and put together a selection that kept things lively. She even saw a few people dancing and was glad to see they agreed with her opinion that some Christmas music was quite danceable. And, of course, Bernie was happy to be getting so much attention from everyone. Wherever he walked, people would bend down to pet him and sometimes sneak him food if he looked at them the right way.

Jake approached Sue from behind and brought his arm around in front of her as he held a fresh single-malt Scotch. "Nice job with the music. I'm hopeless at picking out the right tunes every year."

"Thank you Cowboy. I love putting music together for parties." She gratefully accepted the drink and smiled. "Your timing is impeccable. I was starting to get parched." They stood for a few moments and watched the revelry before Dolly asked her to help bring out the desserts.

JoAnne was nearby and watched at Sue walked away. As no one was talking with Jake, she seized the opportunity and approached him quietly. "Merry Christmas Jake." As he turned to greet her, she felt out of place being there without Dusty. "I know it's probably not appropriate for me to be here considering the situation and I won't stay but I wanted to tell you something."

Before she could continue, he stopped her. "Why on earth would it not be appropriate for you to be here? Regardless of what happened with Dusty, you're my friend and I'm always glad to see you."

The sincerity she could see in his eyes made her feel a little embarrassed. She had known Jake for years and did consider him to be a friend. But when Dusty was let go for his reckless habits and behavior, she wasn't sure if things between her and Jake might change. She was relived to hear him indicate they hadn't. "I just want to let you know that Dusty is getting the help he needs. He told me everything that happened and we had a long talk. He's so embarrassed and at the end of our conversation, he finally broke down. First time I ever saw him cry as he told me he wanted help. I didn't even have to suggest it." She looked down as she paused for a moment before bringing her gaze to Jake's eyes. "I think it's a good sign."

"It's the best sign." He was genuinely relieved. "Someone has to want help before they can get it. I'm thankful he decided he needed to do something before it was truly too late."

She nodded. "I am too. I took him to a place in Bozeman yesterday and got him checked in. He really wants to get better and I think he will. Told him I'd wait for him." She smiled bashfully, hoping that Jake didn't think her a fool. "I think he's worth it."

In her eyes, he could see the deep affection she had for Dusty and was glad she recognized the potential that he and Wayne felt was present in him. "I agree." He looked her straight in the eye. "And I want you to do two things for me."

A quizzical expression settled on her face as she wondered what she could possibly do for Jake.

"First, please tell Dusty that when he's clean, he's welcome back here when he's ready. And second, send me the bill for his stay in Bozeman." Immediately, JoAnne started to protest his generosity. "Don't argue. Dusty has potential and I want to do what I can to make sure he lives up to it. So giving me the bill will actually save me the trouble of making a bunch of phone calls to find out where he is so I can pay it!"

JoAnne could see the sincerity in Jake's eyes and knew he wasn't joking. He would call every rehab center until he found Dusty if she didn't do as he asked. She looked at him with so much admiration, she could feel her eyes filling with tears. She simply smiled and gave him the biggest hug she could muster that ended with a kiss on his cheek.

"Careful now, we aren't even under the mistletoe!" He laughed as she released her hold on him. "Now, you enjoy yourself here tonight. And be sure to check out the cookies Sue made. Very impressive!" He squeezed her hand and smiled as he walked away to check in with Dolly, pleased to know that Dusty had come to his senses.

*****

As the party continued to build, Sue looked towards the entrance of the great room and saw a familiar face. Initially believing it to be someone she met in town, she did a double-take and told herself it wasn't possible for her to be seeing what she was seeing! She stared for several moments as it finally registered that Mark had just entered the room. *What is he doing here?!* He appeared to be with an attractive woman and upon entering the room they seemed to be scanning it, looking for something or someone. Was he looking for her? Had her article inspired him to change his holiday plans and make an impromptu holiday trip? Sue was beyond confused. He had told Jackie he suddenly had to attend a family holiday function. Yet here he was, presumably with his wife or some other girlfriend. *Some 'family function'!* She started marching towards the couple, prepared to demand an explanation as to why he lied to her friend while at the same time preparing some choice words for her co-worker.

As Sue approached him from behind, Mark turned towards her just as she was about to tap his shoulder. He genuinely seemed happy to see her, as if she was who he was looking for instead of, perhaps, hiding from. "Sue, Merry Christmas!" The smile on his face was disarming.

She was literally stunned into silence by his presence and reaction to seeing her. And while she had much stronger words prepared to spill forth from her lips, he had caught her off guard so that the only words she could muster were simple standard fare. "Same to you." Even though she wanted to say differently, she continued with the most non-accusatory of statements. "What are you doing here?"

"Looking for you for one thing. Your article made us want to be here." Mark suddenly realized he had forgotten his manners. Turning to the woman who was with him, he continued. "I'm sorry. Let me introduce you to my sister, Cheryl."

Sue shook her hand in disbelief. *Sister!?* She couldn't tell if he was a great liar or being genuine. She doubted it was the latter. He obviously couldn't have been looking for her or even expecting her to be there. And to so quickly think of introducing whomever it was smiling at her as his sister was quick and clever. And not totally believable. But he so easily spouted his words she didn't know what to think. "Nice to meet you." Even Sue didn't believe the words falling from her mouth. She turned back to Mark, wanting some answers. "Seriously, what are you doing here? I know you didn't come just to see the place I wrote about."

Mark smiled at her, knowing she was probably curious, confused and perhaps a few other choice emotions. "I'm serious. We came partially to see you. And we'd also like to talk to the owner. Your article was very enlightening."

Enlightening? About what? Sue didn't feel there was anything in her article that could have prompted such an impromptu trip for someone who had made so many plans for his holiday with her friend and his actual sister! "I really don't understand. And quite frankly, you can tell me it's none of my business but I'd like to know why you told Jackie you had to attend a family function when clearly you are not. I have a feeling you're about to hurt my friend and that's a serious problem for me."

Mark's expression finally reflected some distress, which gave Sue a bit of satisfaction. "I promise you, that was not my intention and I will explain everything. Really." He seemed to be revealing true sincerity to her. "But first, we'd really like to speak to the owner. Can you direct us towards him?"

She looked at him for several moments, trying to decide what to do. He seemed sincere even if she still didn't believe him to be. But if she was going to get an explanation about what was going on, she decided she had to do as he requested, if only to speed things along. "Don't think you're getting out of a conversation with me later that will end with a phone call to the person you're supposed to be with tonight!" She gave him the most threatening glare she could muster before turning to find Jake in the crowd. Realizing he was probably in the kitchen since she had seen him heading that way just before Mark's arrival, she instructed, "Follow me."

As the parade of three weaved through the crowd, Sue saw a few people noticing Mark and his "sister", seeming to comment amongst themselves. She couldn't fathom why but then, not much had been making sense to her over the last several minutes.

As she figured, Jake was in the kitchen, his back to them when they entered as he prepared to bring Dolly's hotly anticipated Peppermint Chocolate Soufflé to the dessert table.

Before Sue could start the introductions, Mark spoke up. "Hello Dad."

Dad?! What is he saying?!

Then it was Cheryl's turn. "Hi Daddy."

Had she lost her mind too? Sue stared in utter puzzlement as Jake stopped what he was doing, paused for a moment and then turned around.

As if they rehearsed it all the way there, Mark and Cheryl said in perfect unison, "Merry Christmas."

Jake stared in stunned surprise as he gazed upon his, now adult, children. He steadied himself, gripping the counter, seemingly not able to speak. The only sound heard for several moments was the revelry of the holiday celebration happening in the next room. But a different kind of holiday celebration was about to take place in the room where they all stood.

Mark finally broke the silence. "There is a lot to be said and we promise the conversation will take place. But for now we just want you to know we're sorry. We acted like children not that long ago even though we were old enough to know better. But Sue's article opened our eyes. Her words helped us to realize how wrong we were. If nothing else, we had to come and tell you that ourselves, tonight."

They all stood in silence for several moments. Sue was still in shock but felt she had to speak. "I'm sorry to intrude but I don't understand how my article had anything to do with this reunion."

Mark tried to help her understand. "The short version of the story is simple. You wrote about all the things that make this ranch special to Dad, everything that made it special to Mom. And it made us finally realize why certain decisions were made that we were simply too ignorant…or too arrogant to understand. Once I realized you had stumbled on the very ranch Cheryl and I couldn't get away from soon enough, we realized it was time to accept that there were other perspectives to be appreciated in the situation, most importantly the perspective of our mother. We always knew she shouldn't have lasted as long as she did but reading everything you wrote about the ranch made it very apparent to us that she lasted so long for one reason. She was happy here. Not that we made it easy for her." He turned to his father. "Or for you."

Jake had yet to utter a sound since laying his eyes upon Mark and Cheryl. After several long moments spent in silence, Sue could see his eyes welling up as he slowly walked over to his kids and, without uttering a single word, wrapped them both in his long, strong arms, holding them tighter than he ever had. The embrace lasted so long that Dolly had come into the room, stared in disbelief for several moments at what her eyes beheld, then turned around and left without a sound. Finally, Jake let them go, smiling as a tear ran down his cheek. Cheryl reached up to wipe it away as she wiped away her own. And Mark bashfully turned away as he dispatched his own share. The relief all three felt after years of turmoil and misunderstanding was apparent. Jake beamed at them. "I can't tell you how happy I am right now!" He turned to Sue. "And it appears I have you to thank for this."

"I don't think so." She was still in disbelief as to what was happening. "All I did was write about how cowboys celebrate the holiday and things that make this place special."

Looking at his kids, Jake responded. "It would appear that without realizing it, you did a whole lot more than that!" He smiled at her with new awareness of how her gift with words could make an amazing difference in the lives of others.

Sue stared at the reunited family. All she could do was smile as Jake shot her a wink. "Well, I'm thankful if my article in any way helped with this cowboy's Christmas celebration!" She returned his wink.

Cheryl wrapped her arm around her father's waist for the first time in years and started pulling him towards the great room. "Speaking of celebrations, maybe we shouldn't keep you from the party any longer. Your guests are probably wondering where you are. We can talk more later. We're not going anywhere."

Jake could hardly contain his happiness. "Damn right you aren't!" He hooked his daughter on one arm and his son on the other. "Come on, I want to introduce...or re-introduce you two around."

"Not so fast!" Sue mockingly scolded Mark. "I'm not letting you out of my sight until you talk to a certain someone and explain yourself!" The puzzled look on Jake's face reminded her she'd have to give him some background on recent developments in his son's personal life. But Mark knew exactly what she was talking about.

As Jake released Mark's arm, Sue pulled him into the mud room, seemingly the only place where there weren't any guests. "Why did you tell Jackie you suddenly had to attend a family function? Why didn't you tell her the truth? She was really hurt by your sudden change of plans."

"And I'm truly sorry about that. I never wanted to hurt her. But it all happened so fast and if I know nothing else about

Jackie, I know that you two are closer than close and if I had told her, she would have told you and we wanted to surprise our dad."

"And that you did. I'm pretty certain this will go down as the best Christmas Jake has ever had! And I don't want to keep you from him but please talk to Jackie for a few minutes so this doesn't go down as her worst Christmas!"

Mark nodded, knowing she was right. He definitely had feelings for Jackie and didn't want to derail their developing relationship. Talking to her as soon as he could was crucial to keeping things moving forward but he had a feeling there was a good chance she wouldn't even answer her phone at the moment if she saw his number come up.

Sue sensed his hesitation and punched Jackie's number into her phone. After only two rings, she answered. "Hey there, what are you doing calling me tonight? Don't you have a party to attend?"

"I'm calling because I wanted to make sure you answered the phone. I have someone here that I'm not sure you'll want to speak to but I need you to do it anyway. And I can vouch that the story you are about to hear is true so believe it." As she handed the phone to Mark, he mouthed 'thank you' to which she responded with a smile and a look that clearly said 'you owe me'.

*****

When Mark was finished relating his story to Jackie, the silence at the other end of the phone told him there was a good chance she didn't believe anything he had just told her. And she wouldn't have if Sue hadn't initiated the call with a declaration that everything she would hear was true. "OK, I get that this is a pretty fantastic coincidence but why didn't you tell me the night you read the article?"

"Because I needed to be sure. I sent it to my sister that night and she confirmed what I thought when I had read it. Sue managed to stumble on our Dad's ranch! The one we left years ago, vowing never to return. Cheryl and I talked about it a lot and we finally realized how wrong we were and that we had to come here to try and make things right. But I wanted us to be able to surprise our Dad."

"Which I think is wonderful. But you should have told me. I was really upset. I thought we were headed somewhere with our relationship and all of the sudden, everything went south and I had no idea why."

"Believe me when I tell you I am so very sorry about that. I never meant to hurt you because I'm also thinking our relationship might be something special. But like I said, everything developed pretty quickly. My head was spinning with everything I read in the article and wanting to make things right so I probably wasn't thinking clearly." He paused, hoping to let his words sink in. "Besides, the three of you are so close, can you honestly tell me that if I had told you about all this, you could've stopped yourself from telling Sue or Melanie?" He hoped the smile on his face could be heard in his voice. He actually envied how close the three ladies were and wished he had a friendship with someone like the one they shared.

Of course, Jackie understood what he meant. She would have tried her best but knew she would have found it impossible not to tell her friend and she could have made no promises about it to Mark. "Stop being right. It's annoying." Now it was Jackie's turn to hope the smile on her face was evident over the phone.

"And now I just realized that your entire family is the reason I'm not with you and I'm not with Sue for the holiday. I'm not sure I like your family at all, and I haven't even met them!"

He enjoyed her sense of humor, one of her many attributes to be appreciated. And he was thankful she seemed to be over his sudden change to their holiday plans. "Well, hopefully you'll get to know them soon so you can change that opinion."

*****

They stood in the kitchen entrance watching Jake with his kids as Sue related to Dolly all that had happened in the kitchen moments earlier. "I just can't believe I work with Jake's son and we all ended up here! What are the odds?!"

Dolly touched her on the shoulder. "People may scoff but I believe that things happen for a reason. To me, it's really quite simple. God brought you, Mark and Jake into each other's lives to help relieve years of misunderstanding, stubbornness and pain. Jake would never admit it but he has been hurting all the years he's been away from his kids, from their lives. I mean, he didn't even know what they were doing or where they were." She smiled at Sue. "But a certain writer came into his life and made years of turmoil melt away. I mean, just look at him! He's having the time of his life introducing his kids to everyone."

Sue stared at Jake as he worked his way through the crowd with Mark and Cheryl. He was beaming. She thought about how difficult it must have been for him to not have them around for so long, knowing how difficult every day was for her without her parents. She had never been a particularly religious person but she always believed. And what Dolly said made sense. There were too many coincidences involved for all this to have happened on its own. Everything that had transpired made her feel….joyous inside. She also felt an inner peace she hadn't felt for quite a while and realized it had been growing inside her ever since she came to the ranch.

Both women were deep in thought when they heard Jake asking for everyone's attention as he stood in front of the tree. "Merry almost Christmas everyone! I want to thank all of you for being here and I hope you are having a great time. Tonight is special for several reasons and hopefully the start of some new family traditions." He beamed at Mark and Cheryl, then his gaze settled on Sue. He realized he was starting to hope for something that hadn't been a thought he would have entertained just a few weeks before. But so much had changed in such a short period. He hadn't felt like he did at that moment for years. And the feeling started before his long lost children surprised him with the best Christmas gift he could have ever wished for. But this wasn't the time to examine everything he was feeling. He started his speech for a reason and snapped his thoughts back to completing it. "It's about time to welcome Christmas. Dolly's got the hot cider ready but kids, that's just for the adults. She has hot chocolate for you! So everyone grab your drinks and your coats and let's meet down by the barn. It's clear tonight so we'll have a good chance of seeing the Cowboy Christmas Tree Lights!"

As he had been speaking, Sue made her way over to him. Her puzzled expression told him his last comment had the desired effect. "Did you do more decorating?"

Jake gave her a sly smile. "You'll see. Come on and get your coat. I'll grab us some cider." He hurried off to the kitchen with the excitement of a kid about to get a snack ready for Santa.

As guests gathered by the barn, some climbed into the wagons while others prepared for the walk ahead of them. The night air was crisp and fresh and alive with anticipation. The hot cider spiked with spiced rum kept everyone warmed as they made their way to the edge of the field beyond the coral. Sue looked up in time to see a shooting star and quickly made a wish. A Christmas wish! Before she knew it, she was walking arm in arm with Jake on one side and Mark on the other while Cheryl was on Jake's other arm. As they approached the edge of the field, Sue cast her gaze upon the vast snow-covered open space through which a few days earlier they had driven the cattle. Now the field was calm and smooth, the tracks of the cattle having been obliterated by the storm. The moonlight reflecting off the snow made the field glow and she could see a group of deer forging for food in the distance.

As she was lost in her thoughts, Sue heard Jake's voice. "Do you see them Cheryl?"

"I do!" Her voice was giddy. "I never could before, when you tried to show us when we were kids." Suddenly her voice lost its giddy lilt. "Guess I didn't want to. But they really are pretty."

Sue whispered into Jake's ear. "What are we looking at?"

He smiled. "I present to you one more thing that cowboys get to enjoy. Look at the trees to the right. See how the moonlight reflects off the snow that's clinging to the branches?"

She looked for what he was describing. It took her a few moments to realize what he was talking about but she finally understood. "I do see it!"

"I present to you Cowboy Christmas Tree Lights!"

Mark rolled his eyes. "He's still going on about those imaginary lights!"

Sue jabbed him in his side. "They're real if I can see them!"'

He laughed. "OK, so you're crazy too!"

Jake gently smacked Mark's head. "Pay no attention to 'Mr. No Imagination'. We don't get to see these every year. Looks like you brought some Christmas magic to the ranch."

Mark leaned over and whispered to Sue. "In more ways than one." Then he looked at Jake, the father he had abandoned and never wanted to know. *Why?* In his youth, he had always thought things like what they were doing at the moment were so silly and unnecessary. Now all he wanted to do was know all the things that made his Dad tick, what made him happy, what made him...him. Hopefully he could start doing just that...tonight.

Jake looked at his watch then spoke in a loud voice. "It's midnight. May the blessings of this day fall upon all of us. Merry Christmas everyone!"

Echoes of 'Merry Christmas' rang out across the frozen field of white. After they died away, a single voice started singing *Silent Night*. As the second line began, everyone joined in as they stood on the edge of the snow-covered field, singing along with the wind in the trees for all of nature to hear.

*****

The evening wound down as the last of the guests left. With the house finally quiet and the food put away, Jake, Sue, Mark and Cheryl all collapsed into chairs, finally realizing how tired they were. It had been an eventful day. When Jake awoke that morning, he would never have guessed the day would end as it had. But he was thankful for it. "I'm so glad you're here." He looked at his kids, then at Sue. "All of you."

Sue was thankful too, although she wasn't completely sure of the reasons. All she knew for certain was that she felt different when she was at the ranch, when she was with the animals, when she was taking in the beauty all around her. And when she was with Jake. She never had any inkling that the prediction Jackie had made on Thanksgiving might come true. But when something isn't in the plans, it can still happen anyway.

"We know we still have a lot to talk about Dad. But let's save that for tomorrow." Cheryl was rubbing her aching feet as she spoke. "Right now, I need to get some sleep. Guess we should have asked earlier if there is any room for us at the inn?"

"Always. I never use your rooms for guests, just in case."

Mark was surprised by his statement. "After everything, you didn't give up hoping we'd come to our senses one day?"

"Never! You're mother and I tried to instill a strong sense of right and wrong in both of you and look at the results of my faith in you!" He groaned as he rose from his chair. "I never should have sat down!" As he turned off the lights around the room, Mark went to retrieve suitcases from the car while Cheryl made her way to her old room. Sue went to turn off the tree lights but Jake stopped her. "Let's leave those on tonight. I like the thought of the tree being lit and visible through the window all through Christmas Eve night."

"Gotta make sure Santa can see it, right?"

"Exactly! And I think this year, he definitely saw it."

"I agree. It was a great evening. I'm really thankful I stayed."

He moved closer to her. "I'm thankful too. For multiple reasons. But I didn't mean for you to work so hard. I wanted you to enjoy yourself."

"I did enjoy myself! This is a great tradition. It truly was a special evening."

"All because of you."

"Oh I didn't do much. Just made some cookies and helped Dolly keep the buffet stocked."

"And brought my kids back to me." The sincere appreciation he felt was clear to see.

But while she had written the article which led to Mark and Cheryl reuniting with their father, Sue knew that what she wrote simply made Jake's kids realize their father wasn't the unfeeling, uncaring jackass they had built him up to be in their heads. "I had nothing to do with that. *You* brought them back. You read the article. I didn't write anything specific about you. I just wrote about the cowboy vacation holidays at the ranch and about the cancer patient vacation you host each year and how much the ranch supports the town. Obviously they recognized something in what I wrote, put it all together and decided to come here to hopefully get to know you better. Or know you at all. It seems that their youthful perception of you had colored their adult perception of you, which stopped them from really knowing you. Hopefully now they can get to actually know their father."

"I hope so. Because that would be the best Christmas gift ever." He bent down and kissed her on the cheek. "Thank you." He looked into her eyes for the longest of moments, not completely understanding what he was feeling. In a short period of time, this woman had not only managed to reunite him with the two people he wondered if he would ever see again but she had also stirred up emotions he hadn't felt for a long time. And he was no longer certain of how to process them. But one thing he knew for certain was that he truly appreciated the possibilities the day had presented.

Before the moment got too awkward, Sue broke the silence. "Well, I better get to bed. We'll be in trouble if Santa comes down that chimney and finds us still awake."

He came back to the moment at hand. "Not so fast. I've got something for you."

She wasn't at all certain of what he meant. "I thought cowboys don't do gifts?"

He gave her a wink. "We don't. I'll come get you at 5:30 sharp. Dress warm."

"What could you possibly have to show me at 5:30 in the morning? That's only a few hours from now!"

"Then you better get to bed." He hesitated, considering what his next action should be. Something more than the kiss on the cheek he just gave her? Or should he simply walk to his room.

Too quickly for him to decide, Sue decided for him as she smiled and turned to walk down the hall to her room. "Goodnight Jake. Merry Christmas."

"Goodnight." He watched as she walked away, mentally kicking himself. *Opportunity missed?*

CHAPTER 16

Jake had a few things to take care of before rousing Sue and with his outdoor tasks complete, he was excited as he entered the house, still shrouded in the darkness of an early Christmas morning. He went into the kitchen to finish packing the food he had prepared. He wasn't sure when he last enjoyed the Christmas season so much. Not that he didn't enjoy the holidays. But he usually kept himself busy so he didn't spend too much time missing Mary or his kids, and year after year he found himself enjoying the season without *enjoying* the season. But this year his kids gave him the surprise he had long been hoping for but never thought would materialize. And that certainly was cause for his happy mood. But even before Mark and Cheryl had shown up, he knew something was different this year. Sue had brought a fresh perspective into his life and for the first time in years, he felt alive in a way he hadn't since Mary passed. But he still wasn't sure what to do about it. He was a man who typically would analyze the pros and cons of a situation and decide on a course of action. However, lately he had been enjoying a spur-of-the-moment spontaneity that was unlike him. But he liked it.

With the food packed, he made his way to Sue's door, expecting a drowsy response to his knock. He started to wonder if his plan was a sound one. *Maybe she won't be into this.* But before he could second-guess himself, he was at her door, knocking softly. To his surprise the door swung open almost before he finished.

"Merry Christmas Cowboy," she whispered as she stood in the doorway, dressed and ready, just as he had requested.

In the dim light, he thought she looked radiant. "Merry Christmas Cowgirl. I'm shocked you're ready. It's pretty early."

"There is no doubt about that! But when a handsome cowboy has a surprise for me, I'm certainly not going to make him wait." Looking over his shoulder, she teased. "Now if he would just get here, I can find out what he has in store for me!"

Without missing a beat, he turned to leave. "OK, let me go find Wayne."

She burst out laughing, as quietly as she could.

He couldn't help but do the same.

"OK, don't keep me in suspense. What's the surprise?"

"Look at you. You're like a kid!"

"I told you, it's my favorite holiday. And I love surprises."

"Noted." He motioned for her to follow and they quietly made their way down the hall and into the kitchen, where Jake picked up the knapsack of food on their way out the door.

Out in the fresh, cold morning air, moonlight lit the path to the barn where two saddled horses were wating. Sue was impressed. "You really did get up early!"

"This is one of my favorite traditions. Some years I barely sleep waiting for it to be time."

"Now who is like a kid?" She smiled at the thought of Jake watching the clock until it was time ...for what?

They mounted the horses and Jake took the lead as they rode into the still dark morning. The cold air felt invigorating on Sue's face as she smiled, enjoying every moment of their early morning ride. She had no idea what he had in store but she had a strong feeling it had to do with nature. And that she would enjoy it! They wound their way through the trees but with moon not providing much light under the dense cover, Sue was thankful the horses and Jake had good eyesight and knew their way! It appeared to her that they were coming to a clearing but before they broke out of the trees, Jake stopped and turned to her. "OK, we're just about there. Hand me your reins and close your eyes."

She started to get excited. "Oooo, just like when my dad would make me close my eyes before I got to the tree because there was a present waiting for me that was too big to wrap!" She closed her eyes and grinned broadly as she realized she hadn't thought of that memory in years.

"This one is definitely too big to wrap!" He led the way through the trees to the edge of a small cliff, positioning the horses side-by-side overlooking a snow-covered field. At the perfect moment, Jake instructed her softly. "Open your eyes."

Sue slowly opened her eyes and gazed upon the glowing horizon before her just as the sun started to peek over the horizon. As the glow in the sky grew brighter, the cloud formations perfectly captured the light, providing the most vividly colorful sky she had ever seen. She was almost overwhelmed by the beauty she beheld. Multiple shades of red and gold filled the sky as they watched in silence for several minutes. The new dawn revealed deer standing in the field, seemingly also stunned by the beauty of the rising sun. Smiling broadly at the beautiful wonder before her, she finally broke the silence. "Peace on earth."

"I thought you might appreciate this. It's something I really wanted you to experience."

"It's magnificent."

"I come here every Christmas morning to watch the sunrise." He leaned over as he added softly. "This year it seems extra special."

Sue blushed as she glanced at him affectionately for a moment before turning back to take in more of the natural beauty before her, wanting to appreciate it for as long as she could. She pointed to the trees at the other end of the field. "Look at how the sun is reflecting off the icicles hanging on those trees."

"And now you've seen cowboy tinsel. See, we have all the things you city-folk have. It just comes in different forms to cowboys."

"I'm starting to think there is no end to the beauty out here."

"If there is, I haven't found it yet."

As Sue continued to watch the sky change every second the sun rose higher on the horizon, Jake took a thermos from his knapsack and poured each of them a cup. Then he unwrapped something and handed it to Sue. "Are these the famous, melt-in-your-mouth, ham biscuits I've heard so much about?" He smiled as she took a bite and her eyes grew wide. "Wow! They live up to their reputation!"

"It's my cowboy Christmas breakfast every year as I imagine cowboys on the range enjoying a similar feast while watching the same beauty in the sky." He winked as he took a sip from his cup. "And they go down real smooth with my homemade eggnog!"

She continued to be surprised by Jake. His talents seemed to know no bounds yet he was down-to-earth. He appeared to get great satisfaction from simple things and appreciated all that life had to offer. And it helped that he seemed to really enjoy her favorite holiday!

As they finished their cowboy breakfast, Jake didn't want the moment to end. However, he knew if they stayed there much longer he might say something he had been wanting to say for a while. But he wasn't sure he should so he had been holding back, wondering how long he would be able to continue keeping certain thoughts to himself as he swallowed his last drop of eggnog. "Guess we better get back to the house. By now Dolly's preparing breakfast and the guests will be up soon."

Sue watched the sky as he packed up his knapsack, not wanting to leave. But she knew if they stayed there, she might not be able to stop herself from saying things better left unsaid. *Or were they?* She shook the thoughts from her head as she handed him her empty cup. "Well, I'm pretty sure there isn't a breakfast waiting at the house that could top what I just had. Best Christmas breakfast ever!"

"You'll eat those words when you taste what's waiting back at the ranch. Dolly cooks all her best breakfast recipes on Christmas. But if I'm not there to help her, I'll never hear the end of it."

She knew they had to get back but wanted so much for the moment to continue. "This truly was special Jake. Thank you allowing me to share in your Christmas morning tradition!"

He smiled broadly. "Thanks for sticking around to see it. I was pretty certain even a city girl would appreciate this."

"Amazing scenery, excellent food, outstanding company...what more could a city girl ask for on Christmas?" She realized her comment may have sounded a bit sarcastic but she meant every word. She was having her best Christmas in many, many years.

*****

Dolly and Jake worked together to prepare and serve a delicious Christmas dinner complete with a prime rib that would have made the best steak houses jealous. It was a magnificent spread that everyone enjoyed. Sue was thankful the dinner conversation between Mark and Cheryl and the guests was rather banal. A few inquired why they had never met during previous Christmases and both skirted the question well, blaming school or work for keeping them away for several years.

After dinner, a few guests ventured out for an after-dinner walk while some said their goodbyes and went to their rooms to pack as they prepared for an early departure to catch flights or get on the road early the next day. Jake decided that it was a good time for him to sit with his kids and talk. He suggested the four of them meet at the fire pit out back. Mark and Cheryl went to get coats and blankets while Jake prepared hot cider.

With the kids out of earshot, Sue quietly declined the invitation. "This is a private, family conversation. I'm certain there are things the three of you will want to discuss that an outsider should not be present for. All of you should be able to say whatever needs to be said without a virtual stranger listening to every word."

"Don't be silly. You're the whole reason they're here in the first place."

"Now who's being silly? *You're* the reason they are here!"

"They never would have shown up if it wasn't for you and the article you wrote. That's a fact."

Sue was getting frustrated. "The most my article did was help them recognize they should come here to hopefully make up for the past."

"But that's the thing. You didn't have enough in the article about me to spark this sudden wave of forgiveness. You must have said something to Mark."

"I haven't talked to Mark since before I got here. I didn't tell him the name of the ranch where I was heading to do my research. I didn't even tell my best friends. Believe me when I tell you that Mark didn't hear anything from me other than what was in the article."

Jake was more perplexed than ever. "So why the sudden change?"

"That's what you need to discuss with them, which is why I think I need to make myself scarce. This is family business." She was choosing her words carefully, trying not to offend Jake and his family. "You need to be able to speak freely, something that might be tough to do with a reporter around."

He considered her statement for several moments, wanting to be certain he wasn't making a decision based on a snap judgment. Or making it based on other feelings. "I invited you to be my guest for Christmas because I like having you here. And you seem to like being here. I'm not worried about anything that might be said. I have nothing to hide."

It was obvious to her she was not going to win the argument. And if she was being honest with herself, she was pleased to hear him say he liked having her there. He was right; she liked being there. Very much!

*****

The conversation around the fire pit started easily enough with Mark and Cheryl filling their father in on what they had been doing since they had last really spoken. It pleased Jake that his kids had made something of their lives. He had desperately wanted them to succeed on their own and find their true passion as he had been fortunate enough to do in his lifetime...twice. But while he was thankful that moving from the city eventually had the effect on their kids which he and Mary so desired, he was saddened that he missed so much of their lives. Years when they should have been leaning on him for support and advice were spent apart although it appeared to him that his now adult children were closer than ever and had been leaning on each other while estranged from him.

After catching up on their personal lives, Cheryl turned to Sue. "We obviously have you to thank for bringing us all back together."

She did not want to be the center of the conversation. "I really had nothing to do with it."

"Of course you did. If you hadn't written about Dad, we never would have realized what giant asses we've been!"

"I didn't write that much about your father. Just general details. You and Mark put it all together."

"Well, it's really Mark who put it together. Or at least started to enough that he sent me your article. Once I read it, we talked and figured you had stumbled on the ranch where we grew up. Or didn't grow up, depending on your definition of the term."

Jake was thankful Sue seemed relatively comfortable engaging in the conversation she had been trying to avoid. "I'm still trying to figure out how that happened." Turning to Mark, he continued. "Why did you send her here?"

"Believe me, I didn't. At least not intentionally. We were at a party and I overheard Sue saying she was having a hard time finding cowboys to interview. I was just trying to help a co-worker with some information regarding where I thought she could get what she needed. I knew there were plenty of cowboys in Montana. Never dreamt she would find this place though." He turned to Sue and smiled. "Not that I'm sorry you did."

Jake winked at her. "Me either! But how did you end up here?"

"Pure dumb luck! Wayne was the first person I contacted who would entertain my idea."

Jake knew his ranch manager was unique in more ways than one. "Sounds like him."

"So my initial plan was to only report about the Christmas traditions of cowboys but once I learned about all the wonderful things that go on here, I wanted to include some of those details in my article, to make it a stronger piece. There was so much here for me to write about but I tried not to be too personal. I didn't even mention the name of the ranch."

Cheryl touched her arm to reassure Sue. "You weren't, trust me. But when the two of us read the details you did include…"

"And you did include the name of the town you were in…" Mark interjected.

"…we knew who you were talking about." Cheryl turned to her father. "And we finally realized we really put you through a lot of crap that you absolutely didn't deserve. Actually, I figured it out a while ago but was too stubborn to do anything about it."

Mark wasn't sure what to make of his sister's statement. "What do you mean? What did you figure out?"

She looked sheepishly at her brother. "After everything that happened, it bugged me that Mom and Dad didn't seem to have any interest in leaving the ranch, even though you and I just *knew* they were wrong. After all, we were "experts" who knew everything, which just proves we were young and stupid in more ways than one. Anyway, I remembered Dad telling me during one of our heated arguments that there wasn't anything that could be done even if we moved back to the city. Which, of course, I didn't want to believe. But a couple years ago, that conversation started haunting me and I did some research. Simply put, Mom's cancer was aggressive and incurable and moving wouldn't have changed a thing. She'd still be gone. But now I realize that if they had moved, she'd have been miserable at the end. Dad kept her here because she loved it so much. And he let us blame him even though it's what Mom wanted. We were already pissed at him for moving us here in the first place so we just couldn't find any reason to forgive him." She looked at her father with tears in her eyes. She always knew how much he loved their mother and wondered how she could have ever thought even for a minute that he would have done something to harm or neglect her.

Jake stared at the flames in silence for a few moments. "She loved it here more than anywhere. There wasn't anything I wouldn't do to make her happy, to give her a peaceful end, even if it meant you two being angry with me."

Both Mark and Cheryl wanted to say something, anything to express how sorry they were for how they had treated their father. But no fancy words or insightful soliloquy came to either of them as they all stared at the fire. Finally Mark broke the silence of the night. "We really are sorry Dad."

"I know." Jake's simple response was spoken with a full understanding of how they felt. He had hoped and prayed for years that they would come to their senses one day. Who knew a travel writer coming to town would tip the scales.

*****

"It's been quite a Christmas, hasn't it Dad?" Mark and Jake were walking back the house after spending time in the bunkhouse, something they used to do every Christmas of Mark's youth. It was the one thing he remembered fondly but now realized it was just one of many things that were special about being on the ranch. He wished that he had been able to recognize it when he lived there.

"Yes it has son." Jake paused for a moment and put his hand on Mark's shoulder. "Damn it feels good to say that word again!"

Mark couldn't help but smile. "It's nice to hear it again."

"Sue tells me you are dating one of her friends. Jackie?"

"Yeah. She's one of Sue's best friends. And she was not pleased with me when I suddenly changed our Christmas plans by coming here with Cheryl."

"I'm assuming you've explained everything to her since."

"Yeah, she's OK with it. But she's anxious for me to come home so we can at least have New Year's together. But I told her I wasn't sure I'd be back by then." He was torn between being with someone for New Year's who could become a permanent part of his life or spending the holiday with someone who should never have been pushed out of it.

"Glad to hear it. Because I need a favor. From both of you. I want to do something special for Sue."

Mark had seen a similar look on his father's face before and knew that he was formulating a plan for something fun.

*****

After an exhausting but fulfilling 24 hours, Mark and Cheryl had gone off to bed while Jake sat in front of the fireplace in the great room, relaxing as he gazed at the flames and listened to the crackling wood.

Dolly walked into the room and surveyed the scene. She was still finding it hard to believe that his kids were there and once again snuggled into their old beds on Christmas night. "I don't ever recall a Christmas quite as interesting as this one."

"Certainly not the Christmas I was planning for a few weeks ago." Jake smiled as he looked up. "Thank God!"

"I think He gave us a good one this year. First one in a while."

"Indeed." Jake looked at the tree standing in its new spot.

"Lots of changes this year, all seemingly for the better."

"Couldn't agree more." She yawned and stretched, barely able to keep her eyes open. "I'm off to bed. Wake me for New Year's"

He yawned as well. "I'm not far behind you. Goodnight Dolly. Merry Christmas!"

"Merry Christmas Jake." She smiled fondly at her friend. "See you in the morning." She made her way down the hall as Sue was coming out of her room with a gift-wrapped box in her hand. "Goodnight Sue. Merry Christmas."

"Goodnight Dolly. Thank you again for a wonderful meal."

"My pleasure. But I want to thank you for making him smile again." She nodded towards the great room. "Don't get me wrong. Jake smiles all the time. I've never seen someone who smiles as much as he does. But I've known him long enough to know when the smile is something he *wants* to do instead of something he *needs* to do." She looked Sue square in the eye. "Trust me when I tell you he hasn't smiled this sincerely for years."

Sue wasn't sure how to react. She blushed in silence as Dolly smiled, then turned and continued down the hall to her room.

Before she let herself examine too closely what Dolly had said, Sue continued on her original mission. She had a special package to deliver! She stood in the entrance to the great room admiring the sparkling tree, the grand fireplace and the man sitting in his favorite chair. She hated the thought of leaving but the reality was she needed to get home. She had been away far longer than intended and regardless of what might be happening here, she had other commitments. She walked over to Jake and handed him the box in her hand. "Merry Christmas Cowboy."

He looked up in surprise. "What's this?"

"This is what I was planning to leave under the tree for you when I came to say goodbye a week ago. Then the blizzard happened and I got stuck here and you talked me into staying for Christmas and all my plans went out the window." She hoped he was properly reading her mock frustration.

"You're not sorry you stayed, are you?"

"Are you kidding?!? I wouldn't have missed any of this for the world. Best Christmas I've had since...I'm not sure when." She thought of her parents at that moment, of their last Christmas together. Yes, it had been a long, long time since she had a Christmas so amazing as the one about to end. "So, anyway, I just wanted to get you a little something to keep you warm this winter and hopefully make you think of me." She surprised herself by suddenly being so flirty...and confident.

He tore off the wrapping like a kid...at Christmas. "Balvenie, this looks like it might be a good one!"

"It's one of my favorites and I think you need it on your bar. You won't be disappointed."

He gazed at the bottle of 12 year old single malt, double-barrel whiskey with appreciation. Not just for the scotch that would indeed keep him warm on the cold Montana nights, but for all that Sue had managed to do for his family. Without even trying. "Thank you very much. For everything." He looked up to meet her gaze. "I'm not sure you realize just how much you've given me this Christmas."

But she finally did realize. And it pleased her that she had a part in reuniting a family. Knowing there was nothing more that needed to be said verbally, she said all that was needed with her eyes.

The moment had turned more intimate than Jake expected. Feelings continued to stir inside him that he was still trying to understand. Or ignore. Or articulate. So before it got out of hand, he broke the silence. "Your gift won't be here until New Year's Eve."

"My gift?!" She was shocked he had anything planned for her. "Cowboys don't do gifts, remember?"

"Depends on the occasion. And the person."

She couldn't possibly imagine what he had up his sleeve. But it didn't really matter. "Well, I guess you'll have to send it to me because I have to leave. I've got to get home. If my friends are still speaking to me after blowing off everything we do at Christmas, we have plans for New Year's."

A mischievous smile came across his face. "About that...."

Sue put up her hands to stop him from continuing. "No way! You can't talk me into staying for New Year's!"

"Oh, I don't need to talk you into it. I'll just have Wayne surround your car with a wall of snow so high you won't escape until spring."

She acted exasperated but was all smiles inside. "I'll just saddle up Lucy and ride her back home!"

"Thanks for reminding me to hide all the saddles." He was enjoying himself. "C'mon, if you stay, I promise it'll be worth it."

"How can anything outdo Christmas Eve...or Christmas morning...or Christmas day?!?" She couldn't fathom what he might have planned.

"I promise it'll be spectacular."

She eyed him suspiciously. "I know, you probably have the most amazing fireworks display this side of the Mississippi all set to go."

"Not unless you want a stampede for Christmas!"

The puzzled look on Sue's face gave way to a realization that noise from the fireworks would scare the cattle, much as it did the dog she had growing up every 4th of July.

"I promise, it'll be a New Year's celebration that'll top anything you have planned back home." He stared at her with eyes that were full of promise.

And even if she was certain he couldn't fulfill that promise, Sue realized what she truly wanted at that moment more than anything was to stay. But she couldn't let him off too easy. "You truly are a bad influence on me!" She smiled coyly as she turned to walk away. "Now I just have to figure out the best way to break the news to my soon-to-be-former friends!"

CHAPTER 17

Jake walked into the dining room as Sue was ending a call. She put her phone down in disgust and glared at it. Then she gave him the same look.

"I think I saw a similar expression on your face the first time we met. And if I'm being honest, I'm a little scared at the moment!" Something had raised her ire and he wasn't sure he wanted to know the details.

"I let you talk me into staying here through the entire holiday season and now my friends aren't speaking to me!"

"What do you mean?"

"I can't get Melanie or Jackie to answer my calls."

"Maybe they're just busy. It's New Year's Eve. They could be out shopping, getting ready for tonight."

The dagger-filled look she shot him did nothing to ease his fear of retribution. "You don't understand. We *never* refuse each other's calls. Clearly they are pissed and not speaking to me. I should have never let you talk me into staying. This is your fault."

He stared at her, trying to determine if she was serious.

"Oh stop looking at me like that. I'm just kidding...I think. I really am worried that they might be mad at me though."

He felt obligated to reassure her somehow. "Maybe they are somewhere with no signal."

Her depressed mood continued unrelenting. "They both live in one of the most densely populated areas of the country. They *always* have a signal."

He hesitated before revealing why he had come to find her. "Even though I'm pretty certain this is not the time to ask you for a favor, can you possibly help me check in some guests who just arrived?"

"I thought you didn't have overnight guests for New Year's. Just a few friends coming from town."

"These people are special. It's a last-minute thing."

Sue was exasperated. "Why not! Looks like I'm in need of new friends. Maybe these people will take pity on me." She walked past Jake on her way to the grand foyer to greet the holiday travelers with a pasted on smile.

The voices she heard as she approached the front of the house were female...and familiar. As she rounded the corner, Sue was greeted with the sight of Melanie and Jackie standing in the entranceway, arms outstretched to greet their long-lost friend. "What are you two doing here?!?"

"We figured since you are apparently never coming home," Melanie replied, "we needed to come out here to see you!"

"I can't believe you're here!" Sue was staring at them in disbelief.

"I may have had something to do with this." Jake came up behind Sue. "Merry Christmas! Told you I had something special on the way for you."

"How did you manage this?"

Jackie couldn't wait to dish the details. "Mark called and said Jake wanted to surprise you and host us for New Year's. We couldn't resist. We had to see what was keeping you out here indefinitely." Looking Jake up and down, she gave an approving smile. "Now we understand why you ditched us!"

Sue rolled her eyes as she turned to Jake. "Have you met my very un-subtle friend?"

"Pay no attention to her." Melanie chimed in. "She literally can't help herself."

"Oh don't you worry about me. I'm just killing time until a certain someone gets his cute butt out here."

As if on cue, Mark came through the door, walked up to Jackie and without a word being spoken, gave her a deep, long kiss. He quickly greeted Melanie, then grabbed Jackie's suitcase as the world melted away for both of them and he led the way to his old bedroom.

Sue watched them as they disappeared down the hall. "Apparently a lot has progressed while I've been gone. From the look of things, we might not see them again until we are well into the New Year."

Melanie shook her head. "I'll fill you in later. Right now I'd love a tour of this ranch and a chance to get to know Jake. I need to see what has so enchanted you to stay away for so long!"

Sue was eager to show her friend all the wonders of the ranch that had, indeed, enchanted her. It was hard for her to formulate words to properly describe what she felt being at The

Big M but she tried her best. She needed her friend to understand what had been so special about the last several weeks and why she was considering making a change in her life. She wasn't completely sure what that change was going to be yet. But everything she had seen, experienced and felt since arriving at the ranch informed Sue that change in her life was desperately needed.

*****

After the recent Christmas Eve party and the tales she heard of past Thanksgiving dinners, Sue felt the New Year's Eve celebration was a pretty low-key affair, which suited her just fine. The cowboys and cowgirls on the ranch came to the main house for dinner and Mark and Cheryl regaled them with tales from the big city. Melanie and Jackie experienced their first New Year's away from home in years with a meal that included plenty of genuine conversation and laughter and less hustle and bustle. The mellower dinner party provided Sue an opportunity to catch up with Jackie on her relationship with Mark, which had progressed more than Sue anticipated.

"I really think we have a chance at something special," Jackie told her. "I'm just thankful there was an explanation for the sudden change of plans for Christmas. I was worried he had flaked on me."

Sue smiled at her friend, realizing she truly seemed happy and content for the first time since they met so long ago. "I hope your relationship continues to grow."

Melanie leaned over. "I do too. But I'm starting to think he might be a little crazy. Why would anyone ever leave this place? It's incredible. And Jake seems great. Hard not to like the guy."

Sue smiled but made no comment. They didn't need to know all the details.

Melanie and Jackie both felt their best friend had changed since they last saw her. She seemed content and relaxed, which they knew had not been the case in recent months...or longer.

*****

After dinner, the party moved to the great room. Music filled the air as anticipation of the New Year and the possibilities it held grew. Before anyone knew it, furniture had been moved to make room for dancing and the party went into high-gear. And once she started, Stacey seemingly never stopped dancing. When she wore out one partner, she would wrangle another to the floor or just dance by herself. Sue was impressed with the smooth moves of more than one of the cowboys, especially when a line dance broke out. She had never thought cowboys would be particularly good dancers but was mesmerized as she watched them move gracefully in their tight jeans, tapping their boots on the floor in unison with the beat of the music and the steps of the dance they were doing as if they had worked on the choreography all afternoon. Mark and Jackie did their best to learn and keep up with the steps but spent more time laughing than actually dancing while Cheryl and Cowboy Bill just about matched Stacey for time on the dance floor. Dolly and Wayne spent much of the evening together talking and dancing, mostly to the slower tunes while Melanie spent a good portion of the evening talking to Larry, a quiet cowboy Sue had never managed to get much out of during her time on the ranch. But he seemingly couldn't stop talking to her friend. It was starting to look like the New Year might begin with some new relationships.

Having refilled their drinks, Jake walked across the room towards Sue. He didn't know if it was the fine Scotch, the festivities and gaiety of the evening or what but he realized just how beautiful she was in the outfit she found in town after she explained to him she always bought new clothes with which to welcome the New Year. It was her 'good luck charm' and she didn't want to break the tradition. As he moved closer he realized she made a simple pair of pants and a sparkling top look stunning and finally recognized how much he had grown to appreciate and admire her during the short time he had known her. He marveled at the ease with which she fit in not only with everyone on the ranch but the townspeople as well. In a million years he never could have foreseen her enjoying New Year's Eve at the ranch when he first met her on the side of the road. Or even guess that he would want her to be there. She seemed to fit into everything like a glove. The town...his ranch...his life. And she made him look at things differently. He sensed she was viewing her life differently as well. He hoped he was right.

As midnight approached, Dolly and Sue passed sparkling glasses of champagne to everyone as Jake turned down the music, then went to stand next to Sue. He looked at his watch and started the countdown to a New Year, imagining what it might have in store for everyone, including himself.

"Here we go! 10-9-8-7-6-5-4-3-2-1. Happy New Year everyone!"

As couples and friends, both old and new, greeted the New Year with a kiss, Jake didn't hesitate as he turned to Sue, wrapped her in his strong arms and gave her a proper kiss for the first time. When he looked into her eyes afterwards, he found it difficult to read her expression. Was she pleasantly surprised? Interested? Irritated? Not interested? It was only seconds before he had an answer as she drew him close for a long, deep kiss that made her heart skip a beat.

When their lips finally separated, she whispered. "That was nice." She stared into his eyes. "A girl could get used to this."

"Maybe it's the start of a new holiday tradition." He hoped it was a true statement.

As the party continued and the sound of revelry filled their ears, they kissed again. And again.

They were lost in swirling emotions when someone started to sing *Auld Lang Syne*. As everyone joined in singing the 18th century Scottish poem, Sue felt something happen deep within her. A spark reignited, one she never realized had even gone out. But in fact, it had. She wasn't sure when, but it was back and the longer Jake held her in his arms pressing his lips to hers, the spark became a flame. And just then, Sue realized that Jake had fulfilled his promise to her. It truly was a spectacular New Year's celebration. She hoped it was the first of many as her New Year's resolution became making sure the flame never went out again.

Sue Stevens was no longer in a rut!

THE END

Printed in the USA
CPSIA information can be obtained
at www.ICGtesting.com
LVHW020148121123
763661LV00108B/5647